Foreword

Ian Frearson is a relative newcomer to the world of writers. He has developed an arresting style that makes a reader eager to turn the page. His stream-of-consciousness way of witing reflects a mind that would once have been described as ahead of his pen.

His stories are for the most part autobiographical, introducing the reader to a rich tapestry of characters in his childhood, his schooling, in his discovery of girls and in adventures in his employment, notably in mountain rescue. Readers may find their own experiences of life echoed here. Here is a good read for a winter's night in a warm and cosy chair.

When someone first launches himself into the world of writing a book, it is usually done with some trepidation and fear that their work will struggle to find readers. Ian Frearson has no reason to be fearful – he has produced something eminently readable.

Peter Dawson OBE
Writer and Education Consultant

JUST DESSERTS

Good Reading.

JUST DESSERTS

by

Ian Frearson

Published by Peter Dawson
30 Elm Street
Borrowash
Derby, DE72 3HP

British Library Cataloguing-in-Publication data
A catalogue record for this book is available from the British Library

ISBN 978-1-8383404-5-2

Printed and bound by Jellyfish Solutions Ltd

Contents

Contents

Introduction

Some little time ago I was temptingly invited to contribute a couple of short tales as part of an anthology of works produced by our local Church breakfast group (*Borrowash Breakfast Boys*). This was such a thrill and gave me such pleasure I was pleased to be invited to edit the subsequent volume we produced, *Second Helpings*. Such were the joys I gained from these two I am now offering a collection of my own work. This small booklet of short stories comes as tales on a group of topics with which I have become familiar over the years and acts as a release for what I now recognise as a long term longing to write.

This desire came to me unknowingly as a small boy, seriously ill with an intestinal problem, thanks to one of my Aunts, herself a lady of letters and a literary buff, who regularly, during the two week period when life itself was in the balance, sat by my bedside and read or told stories and recited poetry. My subsequent love of the Arctic in particular stemmed from this period. The poem, 'The Ice Cart' by Wilfred Wilson Gibson, has been with me for over seventy years now and remains one of my favourite pieces of descriptive literature.

During my short but lively five years at Grammar School I collected a few more pieces ranging from the Bard himself, William Shakespeare, to Malcolm Arnold and McGonagall to Browning. These regularly come to me during certain moments when I need some mental support. I find I can sit alone, in the dark, in silence and derive great pleasure from these short sections from greater works. We are lucky to have the benefit of free speech in our Country and for this I am truly grateful.

So, to the stories, some from life, some from my fertile imagination and a few are a combination of the two. I would say that where the names refer to actual people, they are aware of their inclusion into this volume and, even if not altogether exultant with the prospect, have agreed to its inclusion. To them, to my Mother who was my constant supporter, my Aunt Gertrude, who was my inspiration and to my friends who have encouraged me and provided so much of the material, I extend my grateful thanks. If any of you are close by sometime and would like a copy autographed, I will leave a pen handy, you can do it yourself.

Lastly and predominantly my thanks to Peter Dawson without whom this small volume simply would not have come to fruition.

The Stories

Mother

I was lucky enough to be born in Alfreton towards the end of the Second World War. However I felt already at a disadvantage since my Grandmother had wanted to call me Robin. As if this was not enough my father's ship was torpedoed a few weeks before I was born so was brought up in a Matriarchal family group. My mother worked full time to keep us, sacrificing many things for me. She always was superb at mathematics and seemed to know the county of every town in the UK. She won prizes at school for both maths and music. She cooked breakfast for me every day before going to work, often forgoing her own so I didn't have to. She was just a mother.

When I passed my 11+ exam she struggled to buy me all the expensive bits and bobs that comprised the required uniform for the local Grammar school. One of her proudest moments during my time there was when I won the school Art prize at GCSE O level. She was a wonderful musician, pianist to me at my singing contests and for fifty years stand-by organist at our Methodist Chapel. She always put others first, insisting I went to sing for local OAPs whenever they asked (usually at very short notice) "One day you might need someone to do something for you" she used to say.

She always gave generously to church "You can never give too much" was her mantra and she was right. She taught me that the more you give the easier it is to do. This came in very handy later in life when asked to support underprivileged children in Kenya through supporting a school and helping orphans to change their lives through education. When I was 15 she was invited to attend a Chinese wedding in Derby at which, to my utter amazement, she taught me to use chopsticks.

She backed me in everything, even when I let her down – after being thrown out of college through reduced attendances she still stood by me and helped me be positive. When I started work I bought her some of the things she had never had. A proper cooker, a washing machine, a fridge. She was so proud and told everyone "Look what our Ian has bought me."

She never lost her sense of humour. For some years she worked for Vyella and ran a machine named Addressograph in the postal office, hence her intimate and extensive knowledge of towns & counties. She bought me clothes from the rag box. She brought home lovely shirts, my favourite of which was white, hand sewn and in sea island cotton material. I loved that shirt and as I put it on I felt somehow different. It was to be my downfall.

One day I arrived home around tea time, badly needing a bath in preparation for an evening of music, dancing and female adoration at the local flea pit of a dance hall. It was only when I came to collect my clothes that I discovered a button missing from my favourite shirt. I asked begged and pleaded with her to sew on a button for me whilst I undertook my ablutions. No chance. She firmly stuck to her guns insisting that, since I knew how to sew on button, I could do it and if I was that keen on wearing it I should have left myself enough time to do it. Some time later when I emerged from the bath I found it just where I had left it without the button. In a fit of pique I had to wear an alternative and left the house in a bad mood. Sometime in the early hours I arrived home to find my beloved shirt exactly where I had left it, still minus button. Determined not to be outdone I took a tin camping plate, punched two holes in the centre and sewed it onto the shirt where the button should have been. In the morning when I arose from my bed it was to find that my enterprising mother had made a button-hole to fit it.

"The Lord gives us what we need and not what we want" she would say. In later years, when I was married and we had a home of our own she spent more time with us as a family. She doted on the children and on my wife too, always taking her side against me. Of course she did. She was so proud of our children, loved them as only a mother and grandmother can and never missed a chance to let me know that. We walked into church one morning, the organist saw us and started to play, as a treat for the boys, the theme to "Red Dwarf". "I like this one" she said. We chose it for her funeral and for our 40th wedding celebration. She never could resist listening to or playing music and in later years must have regretted being unable to play the piano any more.

She was my steadying influence. Without her I don't think I would still be alive. People used to ask if she could stop my more dangerous activities. "if he dies doing that he likes most he has no one to blame but himself". She was my rock. My very best supporter.

So make no mistake there is nothing to touch our mothers. They are fundamentally part of us and we should love respect and honour them with every fibre of our being. They can never be replaced.

Did Jesus feel the same about his mother? I bet he did.

Life, but not as we know it

It is Winter 1972. I have no decent place to live, no money to afford proper food. Life at the moment is tough. It is cold, dark, miserable and I am alone. Every evening I spend more time than necessary at the office until everyone else has left, then creep like a refugee out to my little van. A short trip to the local supermarket brings a little relief from the cold. As I enter the doors the heat hits me like a fist. I recall a similar feeling as I stepped from planes into the balmy heat of tropical nights, but this just brings a welcome change from the shivering and discomfort of the weather or my damp dismal dreary desolate flat that I call home.

I choose a trolley, a family sized one, and almost grin at my own audacity. Luckily they have not yet accepted the policy of having to pay a pound deposit otherwise that would be my undoing. Luckily it does not have the almost mandatory rattling wheel and gratefully neither does it have the inbuilt pernicious Starboard helm. I look round the now familiar setting and choose my starting point. Gradually and methodically, with no real purpose and no preferred route, I trawl from one long aisle to another, choosing all the best, most expensive, attractive looking and favourite foodstuffs, looking carefully at the contents then, once approved, placing them gently and carefully in the trolley. Every single item is chosen with care and deliberation, making sure that this was the most desirable and very best I could find.

At the end of each row, far back into the deepest reaches of the huge superstore is the fresh items enclave. Rows of open shelves carrying displays of vegetables and fruits to tempt every palate. At each pass every item is scrutinised carefully and the floor examined from halfway down the row to see if any odd items have fallen from the displays and onto the hard cold floor. The odd potato, a single cabbage leaf, one lonely brussels sprout. Occasionally there is, joy of joys, a mushroom. How these are cherished and met with such warmth and joy. Each one is surreptitiously collected and pocketed for later enjoyment. At the end of one pass a member of staff waits, looking at me from time to time and carrying what looks like a small brown paper bag. As I approach she steps out and meets me head on. My heart skips a beat, what have I done wrong? What has she seen? She speaks – "Hello, You come here often in the evenings don't you? I have been watching you and I just wonder why you do it?" I feel more like a criminal now than at any other time and look round nervously for a safe route out. I am in a corner as far away from the exits as it is possible to get. My hands are clammy my breath short, heart pumping, head spinning. What do I do? I decide to come clean and tell it like it is, after all, I have never actually stolen anything but the odd scrap that I glean from the floor, so I start.

"My name is Ian, I work for a local construction company and have a flat in an unfashionable and cheap suburb of Chesterfield –" I pause wondering how far can I go, how much I can tell without losing my dignity. I decide that dignity is something I do not have much of therefore nothing much to lose and so continue, "The truth is, I have run away from my life and now I am struggling financially. I do not have enough money to spend on food or heat and light, so spend much of my evenings here where it is warm and dry. My flat is a dump. My clothes are beginning to grow mildew, I spend most of what little I have on cheap food and left-overs that I can use to make soup. When I leave the office I come here where it is warm and dry and to take my mind off the awful alternative. I visit every aisle choosing all the very best of the foods on offer, those I like the best, those I would love to be able to afford. The ones that I know and love. When my trolley is full, I go round..." she cuts in, with a hint of impatience "I know all that, I watch you. I have seen you fill the trolley then put it all back on the shelves again. I just wanted to know why you do it." There is no hiding this time so I just start again.

"Last year I met a girl who, at our very first meeting, made me feel sick with utter longing. I felt that I could not live my life without her. Since then I have thought of nothing else but her. Recently she has made it known that she feels the same way about me and now I have given up my former life, my job, a house, home and wife just longing for the slim chance that one day we will be able to be together."

She looks carefully and long at me. What is she thinking? Does she imagine I am a nutter, a liar, a fool? She smiles and I know everything is going to be alright. She then takes from the pocket of her brown smock a paper bag and offers it to me with almost shyness and adds "Here, these are the scraps that you normally collect as you go round. I have collected them for you and will do it every time I am on duty. Whenever you come in look for me".

Her face softens and blurs and I know that much more and I shall be in tears so I just take the offered bag, return to my trolley to complete my de-shopping and leave. As I sit in the darkness of my cold damp flat I make a vow that one day I will give the girl of my dreams a proper home. Warm, dry and full to the brim with love. It is now 2022 and we have been married for forty eight years. I sit in mellow contentment thinking of the past and wonder if this relationship is going to last. I think it will since I now consider her to be a keeper.

The Journey

There is a school of thought that lives through the principle that it is better to travel hopefully than to arrive. Well, to travel hopefully would be a great opportunity if not a miracle on some journeys. There were many such that I endured during the late 1970s that are worthy of consideration and comment. One, the least clever and the most dangerous antic occurred whilst travelling up motorways – normally the notorious M6 – frequently on call outs to some rescue situation or other in the Lake District or across country towards North Wales. Anyway, a couple in particular fit the bill perfectly and serve to show that it is a very fine line between success and looking a pratt. The travel times to rescue call outs were always more than anticipated or hoped for since lives were almost always at stake and other traffic seemingly deliberately just served to slow us down.

One of the ways we adopted to relieve boredom, entertain younger family members and wind up other drivers was this; We usually travelled in Land

Rovers (stock Mountain Rescue vehicles) so the normal seating arrangement was three abreast in the front, similar behind. When traffic conditions frustrated us and conditions allowed, we would change drivers on the move. The one sitting in the nearside seat (left hand side), would open the sliding window, climb out onto the roof, slide across then, as the one from the middle seat slid across into the recently vacated nearside seat, the current driver would slowly and carefully slide towards the middle seat. This involved retaining one hand on the wheel and one foot on the accelerator until the very last moment, when the new driver slid feet first through the offside window and took over driving. By way of safety we always used piloting procedure and the vacating driver would say "take control" to which the incoming would say "I have control". No harm done, good fun, boredom relieved and other motorists shocked and entertained.

The other had started as a normal journey, albeit a potentially long and uncomfortable one, towards North Wales for a Mountain Rescue Team training weekend. Even before we left Derby we knew it would not be a comfortable trip. Seven of us were crammed into an old long wheel based Land Rover, the day job for which was to carry plumbing tools and equipment. Steve sat in the middle with me at the window seat and "Our" Bill driving. It was Bill's vehicle and ripe for mickey taking. It was spartan in every way, even to the extent that it had little by way of even essentials let alone luxuries. Heating was not readily available but there were a series of buttons, rocker switches and pull stops, mostly useless, that Steve and I tested at random, all to the criticism and increasing rage of the driver. "Leave it alone" was a favourite comment as we asked things like "what does this one do Bill?" answering ourselves "Oh, nothing". Bill was getting increasingly frustrated with us and when Steve pumped one buttons and asked "What's this one Bill?", he responded "leave it alone, that is the windscreen wash". Since nothing by way of water or wash had appeared on the screen, Steve said "But Bill, there's nothing happening" Bill, rapier quick responded

"I know, it's dry clean".

Gourmandising

Anyway, here we are dreaming of yesterday – or a little beyond – with fondest memories of the old Council House Canteen. The real thing that brought all this back was a recent trip to the canteen upstairs in the new and current office where, to my great disappointment, I was offered the choice of what there was at one o clock on a Wednesday lunchtime. What was on offer was – more or less – take it or leave it. No amount of complaining would rectify this, nor would it be fair on those poor opportunists having to run the thing, but what a pale shadow of the old Council House Canteen. I remember one cold Winter's day in 1975 when, having spent all morning out lifting manhole covers, we returned (late as usual) to find most of the standard fayre gone.

Cheffy was not put out in the least "Would you like me to do you something quick" she asked. Always ready for a Quickie at lunchtime we two accepted. What we were offered was "What about something on toast, like Eggs? Cheese? Beans?" I managed to respond at lightning fast speed "That sounds just great" and walked off. Within minutes we were served – yes, you heard it right – served, two slices of cheese on toast, each topped with a perfectly poached egg and surrounded by baked beans. Having wrapped ourselves around this, we approached the till. Wearing the broadest of genuine smiles Cheffy politely informed us that "That will be half a crown each please". Can you believe it? We had each consumed something like 4,000 Kcals for – in today's money – 12½ p each. Now that, as we say in the trade, is value for money.

A few years and many meals later, three great Brittannia's (Frearson, Porrill & Wade) entered that same establishment one lunchtime. The orders went something like "Double Egg Sausage and chips please". "Double Sausage Egg & Chips please" and finally "Sausage Egg & Double Chips please – oh, and a plate of chips on the side". The response to these orders was a voluble "Bloody Hell" from one of the well-known old timers. Shortly after this, apparently on the whim of some Councillor, a regime was introduced that saw small circular plastic tokens being issued. These had to be produced before anyone could be served. Of course, nothing sits easily in the life of your happy author and I was away on holiday when these were distributed.

On the Monday of my return the whole office spent the first hour ribbing me for not having a token and so being unlikely to get any lunch. As the fateful hour approached they relented and one was produced for me to borrow. As it happened it was not for me. Anne (Lady wife and – at the time – student at Bishop Lonsdale) was joining me for lunch. She gratefully took the token and we proceeded along the line, choosing from the food available. On attaining the cash register the operator (who had known me for several years) demanded to see my token. "I don't have one" I truthfully admitted. She went on to explain how, without one, I was unable to have any food. By now a longish queue had formed and plates of limp salad were in fear of going cold. To the distant strains of "Do you want chips with that" I admitted that this was my first day back and asked what these tokens looked like. She turned to Anne "Do you have one luv'" she enquired, Anne proffered the borrowed token and was immediately accepted as a genuine customer, despite never having been in the place before. I shrugged, left my tray of food and offered to walk off. Needless to say my money was accepted with alacrity and three days later, the tokens were withdrawn.

A quote from a Victorian book on handling and dealing with the demented states, "There is little that will deter the cunning lunatic".

EYE [3]

Ivan K Finkelstein III appeared almost, it seemed, out of nowhere. One moment he had never existed in the mundane testosterone and hormone fuelled lives of the attendees at Cholmondsley (Chumley) Grammar School, the next it seemed he was dominating them. He appeared mid-term in a blaze of publicity from the local rag after his father, IKF II, exploded onto the front pages of both regional and National tabloids as the New Regional Executive (that's how the Americans refer to quite ordinary people) of a car production factory in the area.

He – IKF III was tall for his age, good looking and athletically built, with a mop of well behaved blond hair atop an attractively tanned face. Immediately he was loved and loathed in almost perfect equal measure. Adored by the girls and loathed by us – the opposition. Although he didn't need the boost, the attention from the adoring females that made up his fan base did nothing but bolster his already obnoxious confidence and ego. He dressed well, chewed gum, blew bubbles, claimed to both smoke and drink and behaved abominably well in front of all females including those of the staff. His original strut soon developed into a pronounced swagger and he pretty soon adopted the art of walking through groups or individuals rather than round them. He was in for a surprise.

John "Jingles" Joynes was a smallish insignificant boy who had never recovered from an early embarrassing day in the first year when each pupil in the class was asked to explain the profession of their father. When it came to Joynes, he rather swallowed his voice and mumbled out something that sounded very much like "Dstn". Mr Hall, a teacher I came to loath, since I felt he had the complementary traits of no feeling and no subtlety, asked him to "just repeat that in an audible fashion Joynes". Poor Jingles went scarlet and managed to blurt out "Dustman" before seeming to shrink down into his chair and, almost casually, wipe a tear or two from his eyes. Mr Hall grinned at his discomfort and several of the girls, especially, it seemed to me, the attractive ones, gave Jingles a look of pure sympathy, thus elevating him to the ranks of being envied by all the boys.

It seemed that Ivan was destined to continue his meteoric rise to success and worship by the girls, thanks mainly to his desire to enter and win every competition there was. These of course were not confined to the sports arena but extended to gardening, bike maintenance, poetry reading, debating and of course the true track and field events that offered the golden opportunity to shine far and away above us mortal creatures. This, as it happened, was his downfall, but no one at the time would or perhaps could have guessed it, and so the events unfold. Every year the school held a sports extravaganza that was the envy of the surrounding institutions. Included in this was a cricket match that was normally the School 1st XI v The Masters. Why it did not include the Mistresses as well is beyond me and would probably not be allowed in these enlightened days. Of all the players to excel was one Belcher, so named due to his ability to produce loud eruptions of wind at any time. He was a huge lad well over six feet tall and well built with it. He was the 1st demon bowler and delivered balls that frequently beat the eye let alone the bat. Net practice often did not include the actual team as they had special tuition and saved themselves for the match. As a result mere mortals like us were drafted in to allow either best bowlers to hurl balls down at us or to stand proudly at the wicket whilst we sent our best balls down to be thrashed through the nets and all over the field. On this occasion poor Jingles was chosen to bowl. He was not a conventional bowler by any means but had the knack of being able to send very quick balls down. Unfortunately here was where his skill ended since no batsman, and often not even Jingles himself, knew where it would be directed.

IKF III had heard of cricket and since he was more than adequate at rounders and baseball naturally considered himself more than up to the task. He turned out (even for practice) in new whites with a brand new Gunn & Moore bat and his old school cap all ready to show us all how they do it in the great US of A. He managed that.

Following his first few tries, facing a couple of slow leg break overs from 'Spud' Smith, balls that he walloped all over the place, he asked for something a little quicker. "Joynes," shouted Copeland, team captain and up stepped Jingles, his round owl eyes glasses glinting below his old faded cap. One or two of us prayed he did not get laughed at as he was apt to take that sort of thing rather more seriously than most. His short, rather unconventional, run up was almost comical. A little after the style of that well-known and incredibly successful Australian who John Arlott once described thus "And Dennis Lillee begins his stuttering run, looking for all the World like Groucho Marx stalking a waitress." Jingles reached the delivery stump. It was not conventionally a good ball. It went like an express train straight at the batter's body, where, due to the unexpected speed, it made contact with the centre of the batter's chest. He went down as if poleaxed, to the merriment of the onlookers.

Nothing daunted he got up ready to face another ball. This flew outside his on stump and would have been judged to be a spectacular wide in the professional match. The third and fourth balls were almost as unplayable but clearly had begun to rile the batsman, who shouted derision at poor Jingles. His fifth ball was a corker. It left his hand like a bullet, never moving trajectory it was just too fast and before he could take evasive action hit the batsman between the eyes. He fell slowly but decisively to the ground, not to rise again for some time. Belcher was phlegmatic. "Drag him out & let someone else have a go" he shouted, following this by a large loud belch.

Some days later IKF III returned to school for his last day. It seemed that his father was about as popular at the factory as his son was at school and they were off back across the pond. The one thing that had impressed us all about IKF III was that, during the practice, his old school sweater, the one of which he was so proud, had suffered and the large coloured decorative eye in the centre of the chest was now very grubby indeed. No one knew exactly how this had happened but Belcher, always ready for a clever comment just mentioned "We should look up to him a little more now, he is the only boy I have ever seen who had three black eyes".

Holiday

A small thin framed boy sits looking down onto a large yard, where a mixed mob of others are engaged in a rowdy game of football. The bedroom in which he sits is spartan and fitted out to accommodate three others. It is the height of Summer in the East coast town of Skegness and downstairs, unseen by the rowdies, unheard by anyone but the few, a small group of the do-gooders are discussing the isolated child, who even now views the game playing out below with mixed emotions.

This is not the first time that he has been isolated from the rest of the group. Not that he has misbehaved and not that he minded the isolation, but the method and the justification did. Branded as a thief and a liar is not something he ever imagined might occur back when two strangers turned up at his house and made the offer to his long suffering and doting mother.

"We have just come from a meeting of the local Council involved with the well being of disadvantaged children and am pleased to tell you that we are in a position to offer you a free weeks holiday to Skegness for your son." This was met with mixed responses and emotions since neither my mother nor Grandmother had, I felt, ever regarded me as an underprivileged child. Following some short discussion it was decided that I would benefit from the experience, enjoy a wonderful free holiday and meet some new friends from all over the country. I certainly did the first but sadly that was, in my case at least, as far as it went.

The day wears on and the sounds of playground activities from below continues until, at the stroke of a bell, all that sound ceases and the boy knows that tea is being served. He is not too disappointed to miss it since the food here is not up to the standard he is used to receiving at home. It is quiet now and he reflects on the circumstances that brought him to this. The sound of footsteps on the stairs and muted low voices stir him from his reverie. The knob turns, the door opens and four sombre faced reluctant looking figures enter. They stand together, apart from the boy and look at him with unseeing eyes. One speaks and sets out their side of what they see as a problem, basically, that one of the others, a large loud brash London based boy, has accused this one of stealing his purse and with it all his money.

The accused merely looks on with a disinterested confused and clearly upset expression on his thin white face as he hears the fact, presented as charges, spoken out. The others look on with stern expressionless stances. It is clear to see that they have already made up their minds and to them he is guilty of the charge. He knows the truth and that is that he has never touched anyone's possessions. In fact it is he who has been wronged in this way and his few poor pence, lovingly cherished and guarded for a special occasion have even now been seemingly spirited away. The abstract sounds of movement come from below as the spartan tea time comes to an end and boys gradually leave the house once more to resume their time of relaxation by kicking a bladder from one end of the rough surfaced quadrangle to the other.

In the first floor bedroom the interrogation moves on and the accusation is repeated by those unable to know or understand how to extract the truth from the facts as presented. The boy's eyes gradually prick from tears forming in the corners until, overcome by science and emotion they begin to fall in slow thin lines down his cheeks. He knows the situation cannot for him ever improve since the facts as seen and presented are the ones they will stick to, so for him the time of trust is gone. At length the spokesman delivers his final sentence, stating that for the next day he will be restricted to the confines of the property. All trips, luxuries, considerations and tuck shop time will be removed and he will not be allowed to mix with the others. "Luxuries," thinks the boy, when did he last see one of those? He is grateful for the opportunity to remain alone since the majority of the others do not share his background or upbringing. The accuser knows he has wrongly accused someone and not for the first time this week either, so the stage has already been set and the die cast. No one will believe anyone now and the week will pass in mistrust and wariness for them all.

The deal was struck, the pick up and delivery agreed and the journey began. It had not been the sun and fun filled experience that had been promised and reluctantly the boy now accepted that this was far from his idea of a holiday. But if nothing else it will always serve as a lesson in life and that, in later years, would be almost as valuable.

The last two days are spent in contemplation and reflection. He will never be free from the knowledge that someone could accuse without any justification, never be free of the stigma of that day, never again trust everyone as he was taught. When the car arrives to collect him for transport home he is asked all the usual questions. Did he enjoy himself, was he happy, pleased he came, grateful to the staff who looked after him. He politely answered yes to them all and quietly kept his thoughts and his feelings to himself. Never again would a holiday mean quite the same, never again would he trust anyone quite as freely, never again get close to a stranger so readily. For him the teenage years would always be tainted with the memory of that experience and that stigma. When he grows up he will never again visit that awful place.

Samson and Delilah

If ever anyone was misnamed it was he. Samson the Grammar school Gardener. It was he who provided, with a little help from his staff, the fruit and vegetables that graced our tables at lunch time and helped us to aching bellies when pears and apples were abundant. One of his few admirers was Red Hot Momma – the School Cook. Her name? Of course, Delilah.

He was short, thin and habitually wore a scarred, torn, creased and greasy well-worn leather jerkin. That, together with his matching face, did not, to us boys at least, present an attractive proposition. He disliked children – all children, and it was a wonder he managed to produce such a daughter who we boys did find so attractive.

Samson's two loves were simple:- creating wonderful floral displays in the various beds scattered around the school's extensive grounds and the School Cook – Red Hot Momma. Both were extensive, colourful and in constant need of attention. The gardens and orchard of the school provided the basic ingredients for pupil meals and the kitchen provided him with his meals. A symbiotic relationship that was heavily biased towards her since all the goodness by way of food that she provided seemed to do little good to his bodily frame or mental outlook.

Jason Robinson was what most of the staff would have called a trouble-maker. To say that he did not work hard was true but to suggest that he was educationally challenged would be far from the truth. Many were the hours he spent outside the classroom door thanks to his lively comments and disruptive influence on the class and many were the times a teacher would, at the end of the lesson, say to him in passing "And so let that be a lesson to you".

Perhaps some of his most redeeming features were that he had a keen sense of fun and adventure. He lived life to the full. On one occasion he hatched a plot that was both daring and outrageous that could easily have led to severe injury and expulsion. Our form room – Room C – at that time was on the fourth floor. It had previously and for many years been a Physics lab' and still retained the row of thick wooden worktops complete with sinks along the outside wall. The windows from this looked out over cascading greens of lawns that fell away to the sports fields. Directly in front of one window was the top of a substantial flagpole that was located right outside of the Headmaster's Study. It was a situation ripe for exploitation.

Towards the end of the morning school session one day Jason cornered one of our young ladies at the back of the class. He, handsome and dashing, she running to puppy fat with a doughy face but impressive chest. His intension were obvious, to use her in his cunning plot. Hers to enjoy attention from her class hero. Quickly he bundled her into a cupboard at the very back of the room and proceeded to remove her ample bra. She put up a short, ineffectual struggle then subsided into equanimity. It was the time of puberty and hormones were reducing all to uncontrollable wrecks. So it was that the fight she put up with young Robinson was only started when it became obvious that all he wanted her for was her bra. Too late for any further action she left in tears of humiliation and disappointment. Nothing more transpired that day and poor Dorothy had to go home braless.

The following morning dawned bright and crisp with a nice cool breeze from the East as we trooped into Room C to begin the day. At first no one noticed the display but as soon as one person did it spread like wildfire through, not just our classroom but, every one of the rooms on our floor. Outside one window was the top of the flagpole. From its head fluttered an article that took a little time to work out but then became identifiable as one large pink brassiere. The whole class disrupted into hysterics and most of the boys into tears of pure joy at the sight. Robinson was the only one who was not laughing. His joy came from seeing all the rest of us losing ourselves in the moment. A sharp word from the door stopped us in our tracks as the Latin Master strode in demanding to know what all the fuss was about. At the same time some murmuring of conversation from below became apparent. The Head had discovered the plot. Despite his shouts for us to abandon the windows and return to our desks we maintained our positions to see just what was about to develop. Latin abandoned for now the Master joined us jostling for a better vantage point.

Samson's assistant bore a bent body shaped it seemed by a strange twisted frame, short in stature and with a bulbous belly. He reminded us for all the world of Grendel, that larger than life character from Beowulf. No matter how hard they tried, no one could dislodge the article from its place. Robinson's action of jamming it up as hard as he could into the pulley saw to that. After some deliberation on behalf of the small group below Samson ordered from Grendel that he "collect the Large pole ladder". A shrug of the shoulders was all the response he got and several minutes later Grendel reappeared, the said article over his shoulder. It was as impressive as its name implied. Hugely long and with remains of its one time lurid pink paint, it was thrown up against the flagpole and set ready for action. The main problem was instantly and obviously apparent. Despite its name it still fell a couple of metres or so short of the pulley system at the very top of the pole.

Without a hesitation Grendel was ordered up by Samson. He began to protest but was shouted down and soon began to climb until he stood on very top rung, gripping the flagpole, both arms around it in an almost loving embrace. After a minute or so of "what shall I do now" time he was ordered to climb the pole. Gamely he set off, looking for all the world like some grotesque animal character. Just as he reached out for the offending garment a crack like that of a rifle report was heard. For a moment nothing happened then, in slow motion, to the intakes of breath from us and a loud wail of terror from above, the flagpole began to topple. It had snapped off just above the support level and was even now making its increasingly rapid descent towards the ground, carrying the howling form of the Gardener's assistant.

It was now that we all seemed to realise the danger and full extent of the situation and started to worry over alibies and excuses. Even Robinson went pale and looked serious. Just as we imagined the worst, fully expecting to see a corpse any moment, the miracle of miracles happened. The previous day the gardening team had been digging over and manuring beds in anticipation of replanting ready for the Summer events schedule. What a time to thank God for his mercy. As Grendel fell his wail became louder and more desperate. The pole was not falling straight but describing an arc, as the weight of Grendel forced it into a strange dancing motion, then, at the last moment it changed again, seemingly of its own volition, and poor Grendel fell off, descended the last ten feet on his back, arms and legs spread wide. He fell with an audible thud into one of the newly dug beds. For a moment he seemed to lie there on the surface. The silence was palpable, then, the ground seemed to magically open up, in fell his body then the ground seemed to fold back over him leaving just his extremities exposed. Slowly Grendel was helped out of the composted bed by Samson and to our great satisfaction was led away, apparently non the worse for his exciting episode.

A cheer went up from Room C but was quickly hushed by the Latin Master, who seemed almost in tears of relief at the unexpected outcome. Someone remarked how lucky it was that Grendel was unhurt, someone else on how lucky it was that the flagpole did not fall on anyone.

Robinson wondered if the bra would be capable of being rescued for use in another prank.

Road to a Kill

I killed again last night. I don't know why after so long but this time it was different and seconds afterwards I felt profoundly sick. I am not used to this any more and I don't like it. It was a fast kill but not a pretty or clean one, but at least it was quick. If nothing else I like to think she did not suffer. Why do we do it and continue to do it? It isn't as if we need to or mostly even want to. Certainly this time it was the last thing on my mind and hopefully the last time it is ever on my mind.

Suffer – how can I know, be sure, be able to feel a higher degree of remorseful satisfaction? Satisfaction – how could I ever hope to feel any morsel of satisfaction after such an act? I remember times past when I deliberately set out to kill. I did not always follow this to the final act, in fact there were times when I became the stalker-observer, waiting patiently until the perfect moment, until my intended quarry was sighted. Watching and waiting for that perfect moment, making sure that there was no one else close by, no one in the firing line, no one to see the actual act and be able to speak of it to others.

I remember the first time I killed. It had been a well rehearsed act that I had carefully thought out, dreamed of, been through all the possibilities and worked out how, where and when it could be accomplished. In the end it was far less of a thrill and achievement than I had planned or imagined. It is hard for me now to admit or imagine the real reason I had intended to go down this road. Perhaps it was so I could feel big, a man whilst still a boy, to be part of the killing fraternity, to be accepted by those already part of it. So did I achieve this with that first kill? Frankly I don't remember, all I can recall is that I half expected to be treated somehow differently but in the end it was a real anti-climax in every way. No one cheered, no back slapping or congratulatory comments, no well done. Nothing, just casual comments as usual and general conversation. I felt really let down, disappointed, deflated. I wondered if it had been worthwhile and if I would bother to plan it again. In the end I realise that I had become just like the rest, I had been bitten by the killing bug and just knew that it was only a matter of time before I set out to do it all over again.

As I walked through the door back home my wife looked up and without me saying a single word knew something had happened. I looked back willing her to just ask how things had gone at the meeting. She would never really know, never accept the feeling and especially not this time. This time it was the worst I had known and I could still feel my hands shaking with the memory of it. What do I do? Do I tell her everything? Disguise my feelings under another topic, a situation, a fear, a close accident? No this time I have to come clean. So I begin. It all comes tumbling out. The meeting, the setting off home, the corner, the face in the headlights, the sickening crunch as car met body. The final bit was me getting out to see the small brown body smashed to pieces as I stood looking down at the young Hare that I had just run over. I was almost in tears and vowed that in future I really will be more careful with my driving and give up for ever the sport of shooting for the table, it has somehow lost its appeal.

Memories

There was a time when the Council House Canteen was a Tour-de-Force, an establishment to be reckoned with. The Head of Cheffing (someone who has to remain nameless just in case a relative manages to get hold of this) developed a liking for me. One of only two people ever so to do, the other one being Red Hot Momma (my Grammar School cook), who regarded me with almost saintly reverence. "He leaves a lovely clean plate" she was heard to observe, ignoring or in ignorance of my less attractive escapades. Thinking on this I remember with fondness my school dinners. Cabbage, black & strong, like rhubarb leaves, boiled fiercely, served red hot and still crunchy. Proper roast beef, fatty and gristly – and in my case – in quantity. Puddings that deserved a gold frame, spotted dick, huge portions, soft & moist, full of fruit with great gobbets of custard, bubbly all the way through (How did they do that?).

In those days we were obliged to line up outside the Dining Hall – let no one ever even consider uttering the festering term 'canteen'. Tables inside were divided into two sizes, those to accommodate six and ones of exactly the same size that were arranged to seat seven. It was the second year before I learned to ingratiate myself with older boys and select 'pour notre table' those who were poor or picky eaters (all the more for me you see my dears). Another trick was to sit at a table for six then, at appropriate times, instruct 'But I don't really want to go' pale & snotty first years (Snotty's) to "Go and get a plate/dish/bowl for seven". This of course caused chaos when the eventual mistake was discovered. By that time we had – like so many vultures around a carcass – stripped the serving dishes to the pattern, and sometimes beyond.

Before any of this excitement happened we were obliged, as was the school custom, to sing grace. Yes, *SING* grace. Not for us any of your poncy "For what we are about to ..." nonsense. No, for us a rousing chorus of "Benedictus Benedicat" rang our twice a day. A milli-second following the final "Aaaaamen" a hundred or so bums crashed onto oaken seats, often with almost matching legs, and a hundred sets of cutlery were wiped cleanish on ties, handkerchiefs or, as was mostly the case with me, a smaller boy's shirt. One did not complain to Red Hot Momma, on pain of the withering look. I have seen her reduce a fourth year to tears by letting the whole of the second sitting into his secret food dislikes.

Now some of the staff ate with us as part chaperone, part peacemaker/peacekeeper. Of these relatively few were musical, so grace was frequently either delivered in gruff tones of the basses or squeaky shrill tones of the less masculine males. The squeakiest of all was the R.E. teacher, whose attempts to pitch grace was usually received with open ridicule. Perhaps the funniest was old Bob, a Biologist who had retired three times but was brought back to fill in at times. He made no attempt to sing at all, merely uttering a gruff "Bene..." then falling into something undecipherable. We followed by racing through in double time in order to get grub down us all the quicker.

Cook occasionally made a pudding that we called 'Sink a Battleship Pudding'. This was a heavy steamed affair with suet crust that puffed and hissed as it awaited delivery. We loved it. Our school fields at that time included a substantial duck pond. This sported not only duck but usually a few waterhen and coot, plus, on occasion, more exotic species like Grebe (both great crested and little). In order to secure larger portions we confronted a Snotty who was told not to eat SaBP when going swimming, on fear of drowning. One enterprising contemporary of mine took a handful of SaBP down onto the field following dinner and feigned throwing it into the pond. At an appropriate moment he drew the Snotty's attention to the grebe "Look, what did I tell you" he stressed, almost sincerely, "Look what happened to that poor duck". The Snotty gazed in disbelief at the waterfowl with only its head and neck above the water. His mouth opened wide and his eyes grew saucer like. I suspect and fervently hope that he never ate Sink a Battleship Pudding ever again. All the more for us you see my dear.

Not a moment too soon

There was an era, long long ago in the mists of yesterthen, when staff lemminged into the building – and now I am talking Council House – at 08:28 then, at the tick of a tock, lemminged back out at 17:01. Yes, those heady days pre-flexitime, when all men were equal and no women aspired to come down to their level.

People walked around with a proper wristwatch that actually just told the time. There was none of this digital nonsense, where supermarkets / petrol stations / Dixon's etcetera all vied for both popularity and business by offering 99p digital watches that worked well for the first four days, then reverted to apparent Golgafrinchan time zones of 78 past 49 o'clock, through either defective battery power or sheer lack of quality. None of this occurred because they were as yet a figment of someone's furtive and destructive imagination. Fancy being told that you would have to carry a device that could not only fail to tell the time in 24 separate time zones but would also act as a calculator (whatever one of those is), a weather indicator, an alarm clock and in some cases even a radio. Back then the predominance of Timex and Seconda predated the appearance of the cheap Japanese Casio digital beast, notwithstanding their reliability and excellence.

During this transitional development between proper watch and electronic gadgetry came a period when, like most cars of the time, timepieces appeared to have a shelf life of two days beyond their guarantee period. There were a few exceptions like the old traditional Omega, the sophisticated Swiss timepieces and, of course, the classic Rolex, all, not only at the time but remaining, beyond the modest reach of an impecunious party such as myself.

I was busy adjusting the time one day on my modest, yet serviceable watch, when, horror of horrors, the whole winding mechanism came apart. This left me in the dilemma of either trying to push it back in, with unknown consequences, or, leave it out and risk inundation by dust/water/mites/worse. Being of an adventurous nature & willing to risk all, I pushed it back in and heard that satisfactory crunch of destruction where fine precision struck through fine precision. The timepiece of course stopped, so, improved its performance by being exactly correct twice every day. This only served to demonstrate the need for something reliable since I missed so many appointments (mostly with my long suffering wife) that she bought me a cheap (everything is relative you must appreciate) second hand & smuggled Rolex – a proper one. It still goes well, keeps perfect time and serves to show that real quality is a good investment since, although she paid £37 for it in 1976, a replacement version would, in 2021, cost around £2,000 (it was a cheap model).

Take heart from this and remember, there is no present like the time.

The Example

It wasn't as if I had deliberately tried to make myself a talking point or to try to offend the hierarchy of the school. Well I suppose it was, but subconsciously rather than deliberately. Anyway, as the Tom Fool of the fifth year and dedicated devotee of the Art room I was more than happy to ignore the school rules and allow my hair to take on a scholastic rather than monastic appearance. It actually fell below my shoulders at this stage and in 1958 that was taboo. The headmaster completely agreed with this assessment and to reinforce it let the whole school into our little secret at one morning assembly.

He began something like this, "It has come to my notice that certain elements in the school do not appear to understand or accept the school's few simple but essential rules. These are produced for all our benefits and to enhance rather than degrade the standing of the school. Since this affects us all I intend to make an example of those whose actions or lack of them continue to flout these rules and thereby bring the school into disrepute."

We all though he had finished, but no, far from it. "Frearson," he went on "come to the front." Frearson froze in amazement considering what heinous crimes he may have committed, then, stepped slowly and self consciously, amidst the sniggers and snide comments, out to the front of the whole 600 pupils and half the staff gathered in the hall. Headmaster went on, "just look at this pupil, he thinks the rules do not include him, that he can do exactly what he wants with no recriminations. He is wrong." Turning to me he continued, "Frearson, you are a disgrace, you are not here to emulate a girl, your hair is farcical. You will leave the school now and not return until it is shorter by a long chalk." He had finished. More sniggers, ripples of supressed laughter and snide comments accompanied my slow deliberate steps out of the hall, across the lawn and down the corridor towards the top drive.

In a way I was pleased. If that was all he could find to pull me up short on I had got away lightly. I gathered my few scant possessions, left the school grounds and set off for the three mile walk back to Alfreton. Less than an hour later I was passing the drive to my Uncle's farm and had a Damascus Road experience, since there would be no one at home (mother out at work) I might as well spend the rest of the day there, where at least there I would find company and, hopefully, sympathy. How wrong could I possibly be? "What are you doing here?"

came the instant comment as I appeared. I explained the situation and the circumstances under which I came to be sent home. Immediately the situation was grasped, a solution realised and "Stay there, we can soon sort that" was the response. In less than a minute the air powered clippers used for shearing the sheep were brought into play. Three quick stripes and my elegant feminine locks were just a carpet on the floor of the 'place below' – a small room located just below the farmhouse itself. I grinned inanely somewhat self consciously as I ran a hand over my newly acquired stubble and thought 'My mother is not going to like this' – I was right. She was in tears at the first sight of my balding head. But tomorrow is always another day and the following morning I was called up to get ready to face my own particular music.

I stood in the Hall for assembly, with my newly shorn pate standing out like a wart on a Magistrate's nose. My friends thought it a great wheeze, others considered it too far. A few of the girls giggled, others looked on with, what I considered, the tiniest bit of admiration, on which I was determined to capitalise at the first opportunity. The Headmaster was speaking "Not only will I not accept flouting of the school rules but I thoroughly intend to make an example of those who continue to do so and those who find them amusing in any way". That seemed fair to me – sadly he continued – "Frearson, come out here". I was dumbfounded. What had I managed to do now? I slowly made my way through the familiar lines of fellow pupils, slowly through the ranks of the fourth, third, second then first year's and out to my previous position below the stage. The Head looked around the assembled school "This boy thinks he can get away with the abuse I have already mentioned but I am determined to show that he and others in similar vein cannot. Frearson, go home and do not return until your hair is longer." I was flabbergasted, "But sir," I said, "yesterday you sent me home for having long hair and said I had to get it cut, well I did". He did not mince words "Get out boy, GET OUT!". I almost felt like saying "I heard you the first time" but managed to hold my tongue before his outburst went into bold upper case. This was to be the second of a few times that he lost his temper with me and all I could do was to roll with the ride. He did not like me for some inexplicable reason and that was made plain at Speech Day in 1957 when, through gritted teeth and in front of the whole school, staff, parents and visiting dignitaries, he was obliged to announce "and the School Art Prize goes to – Ian Frearson".

Game set & match I thought.

Dear Old Friend

One of the hymns I remember and love from my childhood is the one that starts "I have a friend, oh such a friend, he loved me e're I knew him...". One of my oldest and dearest friends is the one who taught me to sail. How could I ever forgive him? Together and with various supplementary crews we have cruised almost every inch of the Norfolk Broads' waters together with a fair proportion of the land adjacent. We also spent time at many other locations all under canvas. He played the organ for our wedding and I was best man at his (very best I remember telling him). Together we have spent some weeks helping out at Girl Guide Summer camps and still have the scars. We do not see enough of each other nowadays and last year, together with his card, I sent him a Christmas letter.

Dear Admiral (Youth)

There was a time when men were mere boys and girls were just a pain in a Guide uniform. We received this card yesterday and it reminded me of some of those heady days we spent together entertaining and being entertained by those self same smooth skinned little tykes with the doe eyes and the scheming minds.

I am sure I recognise the two fishermen in the skiff but feel the dinghy is all wrong and should of course be a Mirror. Do you recall this? Am I wrong or just growing old?

Anne reminds me that a certain latrine digging exercise was all worthwhile but shows no sign of remorse that she could not take part in the filling in of same. I however do recall the decanting of liquor and the joyful laughs of the open topped cars as they approached the watersplash. I also recall the cries of loathing as they sloshed through all that sewage liquor that barred their path in the road below. How happy we made them feel.

I remember too the little camp fire we organised and executed, particularly the way it loved its own involvement so much it remained burning for three days. I sometimes wonder if the farmer regretted allowing us to use his tractor & trailer to collect the wood and if he misses those lovely telegraph poles we cut up & burned.

I think on the time we made a spectacular landfall on Caldey island opposite Tenby and the

DUKW attendant rushed over to inform us that we were not allowed to land as it was a private island. How we laughed as he explained that "only the Abbot could give permission to land" and when you suggested that permission would be sought he retorted with "He never gives anyone permission". Your swansong was the final sentence of "well you're too late anyway, we've already landed" and so we had.

I also wonder if you ever did get your pyjamas back from those innocent looking life loving little mynxes and think often of the day your press studs came out for an airing. How we loved every minute of our own embarrassment.

Who could ever forget the fun and joy of breaking down on the way home with a roof full of boat and steering rack full of shattered casting?

Is it just me or were those days something special?

Remembering fun times spent together and with others who, unlike us, should have had more sense.

Ian (Commander of the Fleet)

Warming up to the Cold

There has recently been a positive explosion of posters and photographs advertising the demise of the planet due to – what is claimed to be – global warming. Many of these feature that most enigmatic and gorgeous creature the Polar Bear. *Ursus Maritimus* or Sea Bear is its Latin name, and particularly apt it is too, although in high latitude circles it is known more appropriately as Ice Bear. I know a man who has, some fifteen times during the past thirty years, been privileged to spend some precious time near (on occasions too near) these lovely creatures.

He has been so close as to have one in camp for a few days and robbing food from tents, had one walk by him as he sat on the outdoor 'panoramic view' toilet and, as if that was not enough, been attacked by one that wanted to take, kill and eat him for breakfast. In short they are magnificent, impressive, powerful, graceful, totally at home on land or in the water and can frighten the crap out of a mere man. They can outrun a horse, outthink a seal, outfight anything, have no natural enemies and no fear of anything. This incredibly includes fire, since they do not come into contact with it so have neither fear nor understanding of it at all.

Despite all this I cannot but think that these posters are somewhat misleading. All the hype over Global Warming should really be completely renamed Climate Change since, in the long term, who amongst us really does know what the future has in store. What, for most, may well be long term warming could well be, for some at least, cooling. One forecast has the prediction for regional snow in Scotland sometime during the next 50 to 200 years. This would see the return of glaciation and all the changes that it entails.

But what of the bear? Well, one school of thought says it is likely to disappear completely through total loss of habitat. Now although this would be a real shame it would not, as some imagine, see the extinction of a species. This magnificent creature has evolved over many years through the creation of the very habitat that is now threatened. Originally the Ice Bear (indulge me gentle reader) were big, brown and living around the northern fringes of Canada and what eventually became Russian Alaska. Their continued association with and residence in regions of snow & ice, together with a change of diet to accommodate the local pantry (sea mammals) required not only stealth, cunning, guile and immense resilience, it also made a lot of sense to blend into the background. Since this comprised mainly snow – a medium of blues and pinks – the nearest that could be achieved was white, so that is precisely what happened and one branch of the Grizzly Bear gradually turned into Polar Bear.

Their nearest cousins, the Kodiak Island brown bear, are enormous, as large as their white relatives, and occur in the region we visited in 1981. A local asked if we were familiar with bear and we all had to admit no. "Well," he began "there is a difference between black and brown bear (Grizzly Bear). If a black bear attacks you and you climb a tree, he will climb up after you and kill you. The brown bear won't". "Blimey", said one of the group, "In that case, give me a brown bear anytime." There was a short pause before Joe went on "No – the brown bear will just push the f'kin tree over & eat you anyway".

So, if the polar Bear do all die out the thing to do is to look out for the return transition that would herald the return of a cooler global climate, when once again polar ice returns as a complete unbroken annual sheet, brown bear turn white and men are, once again, able to be scared to death by this magnificent creature. After all, it should not take more than a few hundreds of thousands of years.

Always providing man lasts that long of course.

Albert

My Auntie Winifred was the oldest of my Aunties. Her Husband, Bernard – after whom our eldest was named – was a professional gardener and groundsman. His duties included the gardens of five substantial houses (all the gift of a self-made millionaire from Alfreton, who emigrated and found his fortune in America). The rest of his duties lay in the upkeep and maintenance of some acres of lawns, several ash tennis courts and a beautiful crown green bowling green, all accompanied by lovely bright and spectacularly laid out flower beds.

Their first offspring, a vivacious and attractive young thing who they named Audrey, tragically died shortly after giving birth to her son, my second cousin Michael. Their second, another daughter, who they named Winifred, could not have been more different and was cool, introverted, very staid, quiet and reserved. She grew up to marry a man called Albert, and now gentle reader, you have been introduced to the object of our story.

Albert had his own greenhouse. A modest but to me an exciting affair in which he tended nurtured and grew over four thousand cacti and succulents. Some of these were magnificent, all were definitely classed as anti-social and a few were actually poisonous so treated with the greatest of respect. Many of them flowered annually in the most exotic, spectacular but disappointing manner imaginable, with the flower emerging late evening then dead by the following afternoon. Albert tended to them dressed always in his old battered leather jerkin, looking for all the world like some Medieval squire, lovingly sorting and polishing his Master's armour. I loved being with him and the cacti in equal measure so would happily sit quietly in a corner just watching him trim, weed, divide and occasionally jettison the various plants as needs took.

Prior to his current position he had worked for The English Sewing Cotton Co. at the mills in Belper. These were formerly part of an empire owned by the Strutt family and well known throughout the world as producing thread of excellence. The location of their mills, on the banks of the River Derwent, was not accidental and allowed them to install a revolutionary new concept in power by the combined means of water wheel direct from the river and electricity through the turbines, again harnessing the power of water. Albert, never an academic, was engaged in a series of activities, including greasing, adjusting and maintaining both systems and patrolling the river. This last was the one that enthralled me and some of his tales had me on the edge of my little stool – another result of his habit of making the odd item from left over materials. During times of heavy prolonged rains – the standard of winters during the 1950s – one of Albert's jobs was to ensure that no debris washing down the swollen river came close to threatening the safety or performance of the waterwheels or turbines. In order to do this he was given, or more correctly, allocated, a rowing boat with a pair of long shapely oars. To his delight the boat simply flew across the water under his muscular arms and frankly he slightly abused the privilege of his position by taking it out ever so slightly more frequently than was strictly necessary. A side bonus of catching up and removing the various branches and sometimes whole trees that carried themselves in a grim rotating dance downstream was that very occasionally a body would accompany them. These varied, from some poor unfortunate who had simply slipped and fallen in, to the dedicated suicide victim who had deliberately changed his life forever by sliding into the unforgiving waters of the flooding river.

One particular day in mid December 1957 he was gazing out of the little window in his tiny office when he spotted a bowler hat whirling and turning in a familiar macabre dance downstream.

Albert had always fancied himself wearing a bowler and saw this as his best chance. He had been out many times in floods worse than this, so without considering the condition of the flooding river he skipped lightly down to the boat house, ran his little skiff into the water and, taking the oars in hand, set off with powerful strokes, rowing crab like towards the hat, now bobbing and dancing its way towards the weir. He knew he had to be fast and before arrival had already worked out his strategy for collecting the prize and getting back to the bank safely. Rounding up just downstream of the hat he skilfully reached out and made a grab for it. Strangely it seemed to be much heavier than he had envisaged or anticipated. Tugging more firmly it eventually came free and popped off the head to which it had been attached. "Bonus" thought Albert, as an additional bonus of the job was, he retained a bounty for the body of each poor unfortunate he managed to remove from the river.

It was then that an awful thought struck him, was the man actually dead. He imagined rather than saw his victim make a strangulated gasp then roll over again to lie face down in the flow. It was then, conspiratorially confided to me, that he thought the unthinkable. For successfully rescuing someone who survived he would receive nothing. For a body, the bounty money of one crown (five shillings – or more correctly nowadays, twenty-five pence) and for one moment considered holding off a minute or so until his bounty was guaranteed.

I sat transfixed with eyes like saucers. "So what did you do?" I managed to gasp. He looked at me sagely with a serious expression and simply said "Well what would you do faced with a situation like that", then, with a whistle and a light swing in his step he walked off to another little job in the garden, wearing on his head a slightly battered and grubby bowler hat.

Christmas Dinner

It was a mere four years ago when our daughter (by then a married woman with a home of her own) last crept into our bed at impossible o'clock Christmas morning demanding that we open things from our Christmas stocking and merge it with enjoying a satsuma or an apple – or how about some chocolate money, or even a nut or two. We had by this time managed to restrict her to appearing 'not before eight-o'-clock' and she was always spot on the button. This delightful tradition has been enjoyed by us and families before us for generations so is nothing new. Our boys too used to be there before it was light, snuffling through their stockings like so many swine amongst fallen leaves (these stockings were always my hill socks, since I had the biggest in the household) searching for tit bits and those cheap little plastic stocking fillers their mum took such a delight in finding. Bright excited little eyes would locate another £1.00 element and extract it with both genuine glee and their small shrill voices demanding our attention to this new discovery. What delightful times we had for many years, with fond memories of similar happenings in our own childhood, which in turn no doubt stimulated similar memories for our parents – and so on back and back.

I remember lonelier times too. Days when, around this most festive of seasons, I slept alone and cold, dreaming of my heady childhood days and longing for company. It came back to me when really needed. My wife Anne likes tradition at Christmas and she always enjoys in every way the standard traditional Christmas Dinner. Turkey of course, needless to say stuffing of numerous alternative varieties, creamed potatoes, roasties for the piggy-wigs, roast parsnips, carrots, Brussels sprouts – a definite must in our house since at least one of the family demands it – these with bacon bits and marrons (chestnuts), pigs in blankets, bread sauce and of course a really rich succulent gravy. None of this whispy thin sauce lark, gravy, proper stuff, and so it goes on. I may well have missed something, I usually do, but then again, does it really matter, after all, the object of the exercise seems to be to fill oneself so full that even breathing can be a challenge.

I remember one particular Christmas Day when, having eaten myself to a standstill, I lay on the dining room floor groaning and clutching at my stomach. Anne had no sympathy. "Come on, get up, we are going for a walk" she started. At last, I made the move and within ten minutes was really glad I had made that effort. My mother was not so generous. "Ooh our Ian," she said, "You'll make yourself ill eating like that". She had the perspicacity of something really perspicacious that woman.

Unlike my lovely wife, I go in for something a little less traditional if not challenging. Poached salmon, roast wild boar, venison, guinea fowl, peacock, goose and duck have all featured on my alternative Christmas dinner menu. We take it in turns to cook the actual Christmas Day dinner, so no one feels they are left out. Admittedly there has been the odd occasion when my dinners have been accepted with less than enthusiasm but generally they have been a hit. I remember one particular occasion when I had managed to obtain a really nice haunch of venison, aged it to perfection, marinated it to the succulence it would retain throughout and cooked it to exactly my sort of underdone state. I sliced it in the kitchen plating up as I went. The children have always been used to us eating our own chickens from the bottom of the garden so to them meat is just that, but one plate had to receive just that little extra attention. Just before I brought out the one specially prepared for our daughter I gently and carefully placed half a maraschino cherry on the centre of the meat.

As I placed it before her on the table I said softly to her "look darling, you lucky girl, you have got Rudolph".

Last Day

The cell is dark and inhospitable. No sound but the ragged breath of the single inhabitant disturbs the silence. A young man is draped across a narrow hard cot. In one corner a bucket latrine stands part full, the contents cold. The man's clothes are thin, poor, hardly adequate for the conditions. It is cold, dark, singularly unattractive. He keeps reminding himself of that and of one other thing. Words continue to come into his mind and his mouth. "He must come. He Must Come".

It is the 1950s and Capital punishment has not yet been repealed. Sadly, for this young man it will come just too late. He knows it. He also knows just why he is here, and this is the driver that compels him to maintain his requests for this particular person as his final visitor. On arrival they had asked the usual questions including "Faith?", to which he had replied "None", not as a declaration of no faith but as his final admission that having lost all faith has become almost everything. There are sounds outside the door, his heart rate increases, his mind rushes forward with scenes, hopes, fears. There is the sound of a key scraping and turning in the lock and the bark of an order to stand well clear of the door. He does. As it opens he begins to see glimpses of those outside. Two are familiar to him. The one is tall, gaunt and steely silent. He brings food at regular intervals but utters no word. Not one single syllable. There is no hope there. The second is a large muscular man who carries and operates the keys. He speaks occasionally but never in a positive way. The third he can't yet see. He hopes, he hopes, he even begins to beg, almost to pray. As the steel door swings slowly and monotonously wider the third man begins to be revealed.

We go back a little. It is 1951 and our young man is a late teenager with all the problems and benefits that this age bestows. He is naturally fit. Lean and wiry with a relaxed loose gait that gets him attention from the girls. His long blond hair and fair skin is the envy of many, and he has one more major trait that lines his dish of life with the pure gold of butter – he remains unspoilt by it all. The invitation to the wedding of a relative comes as a complete surprise but welcome break from the usual tedium of the weekend routine. His family are steeped in Methodism so it will be a simple but joyous occasion. The post service celebration continues at a local Hotel into which he has never before stepped. It is plush and warm. Welcoming but obviously slightly above his usual haunts. The hubbub and trappings of the wedding and its guests surround and cocoon him, particularly the bridesmaids and friend of the bride who eye him with looks bordering on rather more than admiration. He likes it. The breakfast and speeches completed the accumulated guests drift about and relax whilst the room is prepared for the buffet and party. Conversations vary from family matters to plans for assignations and dates to book and remember. He is in his element with no shortage of pretty young things paying him some attention. Amongst the guests is the Minister who performed the marriage ceremony. He is so unlike the traditional view of a man of the cloth, round jovial and full of mirth, he quickly fits in with the party and is soon enjoying a glass of beer, then wine, punch and whisky, seemingly without it having any effect on him at all. He appears to be an altogether good egg. He smiles a lot.

This third man is soon revealed as the minister who now has a more sombre expression and appears not to be aware at all of the reason why he has been called to attend this desolate, dark, dank, depressing place. Nonetheless he enters the cell and faces the young man. For some moments no one speaks. The two relative strangers observe each other carefully. At last the young man starts with his planned and well rehearsed opening gambit – "You don't remember me do you?". The sombre faced Minister looks embarrassed confused, outside his comfort zone. The young man continues – "You are the reason I am here". A sharp intake of breath from all the newcomers breaks the silence of the cell. A look of shock crosses the Ministers face, but it is the young man who continues – "Yes, you remember ------ & ------[1] who were married in Spring '51, well that is where you started our plan. Let me explain.

I was brought up in a Methodist household with strict moral and ethical code and until that day had never before tasted or tried alcohol. I never really wanted to. I had been taught about the dangers of drugs. That day I saw how apparently happy and content a drink made you, so thought it might do the same for me. I tried it, I liked it, I tried some more and the more I tried the better it seemed to be and the more I wanted. That summer I was out every night with my so-called friends drinking and having a good time. You remember the chief bridesmaid? Perhaps not, well I did, and I was well impressed. I wanted her and thought she wanted me. One night I got so drunk all I could think about was her and how much I wanted her. Problem was, it turned out she didn't really want me – not in that way. She tried to stop me, she fought and scratched me, kicked me punched me and that really upset

---

1   It would be unfair and crass to mention names at this juncture so make do with your imagination

me. I can't remember how it happened, but I tried to stop her shouting. It worked. Problem was Vicar, it stopped her breathing. She looked so calm, but she was not going to move again. So now here I am and it was seeing you at that wedding that made me feel I could start to drink. Well now here I am, thanks to you.

The Minister blanches, his shoulders droop, his head bows, he starts to cry.

Cry away my friend, cry away, it is too late for tears, too late for remorse, too late to set an example. You unwittingly set an otherwise sensible young man on the route to the gallows.

Please remember him on Sunday when you pray to your god.

This is his last day.

Lines on Cycling Equipment

The office window lies ajar and yet
The rank and foetid smell as of death rides still
along the corridors
Of desks that map out the layout of this dull and
awkward room.

So where is he that striking and dynamic figure,
in hugging lycra and Nike shoe who, with
purposeful stride
and fitness oozing from every pore, and
whose pose
demands attention without uttering
one single word.

He is gone, scattered remnants of his presence yet
still adorn the chairs, the desks, the floor, from
where, in casual attitude,
his rucksack slumps in silence and without a
morsel of elegance.
He will return and then, the room will light up
once again.

But now, his presence could not be more
confirmed but less desired
for he is here in olfactory offence alone.
That man of whom they speak so well.
Donaldson – it is he.

Tony Donaldson and I met at an outside meeting of
Developer and Authority to talk some sense about
limiting the flows of surface water into an already
overcharged system. Tony spoke little but smiled a
lot when we challenged their proposals and some
more when we casually dropped out our intentions
to prosecute anyone considered sufficiently unwise
to deliberately pursue proposals that could see
properties inundated with surface water. They
backed off, and Tony – their Consultant Drainage
Expert – reprogrammed their proposals to meet
our requirements. Result. Three weeks later Tony
came to the office and asked if we were looking for
staff. We were and I was. He made such a difference
to the Team and brought a professionalism to our
office that made it a sheer pleasure to come to work.
He quickly fitted in, to the extent that he became
a friend and attended social events (initially band
concerts) with his girlfriend, Badger. Now don't
get the wrong idea. Badgers, one of my favourite
animals, are wide in the aft beam, short sighted
and snuffle a lot. This one was none of these. Slim,

lithe, attractive and young, she is the antonym of the other animal. The only way in which she could possibly be said to resemble one is that she has a series of streaks in her hair. Let me tell you, they are lovely enough on the animal, on Catherine they are such that they make her stunningly attractive. So next time you are listening with half an ear to a conversation and think you hear me say "Yes, he and Badger came round to a meal..." you have no need to check your hearing or look round for Ratty or Mole, it's just me talking honestly about people that I choose to have around me. If on the other hand you happen to be in Shipley Park one day and she comes racing past, undertaking her best Nordic Walking, then you can come home and honestly say "I was overtaken by a badger today"

November

November, month, for me not of mellow fruitfulness but of melancholy. How, in the name of Jupiter, did it return so very quickly this year? I have a theory that it stems from the lack of seasonal delight normally known as Summer. Whatever the reason, November has appeared and, almost as quickly, disappeared in favour of the Festive month. I remember as a callow youth making daily journeys to and from Derby and the most memorable occurred during the month of November. It stands out like a wart on a magistrate's nose, being the time that coal fires were at their apogee and smog recognised as a major health hazard.

In those days everyone smoked, either actively (Park Drive for the mobs, Senior Service for the nobs) or passively, thanks mainly to British Coal, with a myriad of chimneys belching out acrid yellow breath. So, one Thursday evening at nine, I looked forward to my thirteen-mile journey home from Art School in Derby to the modest household in Alfreton. Without wanting to hurl myself on the sympathy of the stony hearted, I would only add that these journeys were, through enforced circumstances, secured by thumbing a lift. There were good days and bad during this period. On good days I was picked up by one of my regulars, one of whom was a headmistress. On bad days, I arrived home in the early hours, cold, wet and miserable, with similar prospects promised for the next day.

On this particular occasion I walked out of college into a world of the cold wet blanket. It was impossible to see the kerb edge from the building. Resigning myself to the worst I set off, walking with one foot on the kerb, the other in the channel, so as not to lose the footway edge. By instinct and some experiment I arrived opposite the Council House. Knowing this area well I set off directly across the road, heading for Journey's End, a transport café on the Alfreton Road. After a few seconds fumbling in the grey blanket I fell over something. At first I thought it may be a car? No, it was too small. A body? Too hard. I felt around. It turned out to be the roundabout in the middle of the road.

Just after ten o' clock I had made the café at the very moment a lorry driver came out and approached his vehicle. "Are you going towards Chesterfield?" I asked. You would have been forgiven for imagining that I was his long lost brother, so grateful was he to have someone else in the cab. So, in I climbed, off we set. It was not a pleasant journey, with each of us hanging out of a window, eyes seeking an edge. In my case, the kerb, in his, the white line. I recognised the start of the dual carriageway section towards Little Eaton and imagined us home and dry. In those days Halogen lamps were still a thought in some unborn mind, six Volt systems still abounded and the soft dull orange glow from lamps pooled unwillingly on the ground.

The edge of a layby appeared and I warned my benefactor. "Good" he said, and we pulled in. "Let's clean the lights" he suggested, jumping out and handing me a cloth. He started with the important ones, I took the stern. As I felt my way to the rear of the vehicle, at least two sets of headlights suggested that we were not the only ones to have stopped. I was wiping lights clean as a plummy voice came out of the heavy sulphurous ether "I say, is it a bad accident?" At first it did not occur to me that this was addressed in my direction. Some seconds later three groping figures approached and asked if the road was completely blocked. At last the penny dropped. In those days pennies were something, so dropped well. Behind us was a crocodile of vehicles that were blindly and faithfully following us.

This in turn led me onto thinking about annual November celebrations. The fifth, with increasingly explosive and impressive pyrotechnics, closely followed by the 11th, with the quiet services of remembrance. My mother served in the services during the war. So did my father, who I never knew, since his ship was torpedoed and sunk off Malta some weeks before I was born. So now, I began to think of all the millions of men who blindly and faithfully followed the demands of their sergeants, officers, ministers, parliament, King and all in the name of a good cause. As the years have gone by, the act of remembrance has become more important to me, so we never forget what others did on our behalf. At one of the services recently, when I was suggesting to a young thing that we might be serious for a couple of minutes, a pompous gentleman (I use the term loosely) turned to me and asked "So what did your father do for us during the conflict then?" "Died" was all I could bring myself to admit.

See you in Court

The time was the Nineteen Eighties and it was a young and fiscally impecunious party that had accepted the kind offer of a twin tub washing machine from his in-laws. All went well until, one day, little wifey complained that the spinner no longer spun. The presence of one tiny addition to the family circle was proving to be harder work, totally out of all proportion in fact, than had been envisaged at the 'agreement to embark' stage. The problem was duly reported to said donor and the news came back that scarcely three months ago the machine had been serviced and a brand new spinner motor, with a one year guarantee, had been fitted. Deep joy, the contractors had been the Electricity Board themselves, so no problems were envisaged there, a quick phone call would fix it.

The call was made, the appointment agreed, the man turned up. "I have a bad back" was his opening gambit "Could you move it out into the open," quickly followed by "Could you tip it up for me now?" The machine was duly turned around and tilted so the underside could be examined. Immediately the problem was clear, one of the power wires to the motor had come off the fitting and that was all it would take to restore it to full working capacity. This was pointed out to the fitter. He was not a man to be put off his job by anyone so practical. He decided that it would be easier to fit a new motor. Young Lochinvar stuck to his guns telling him that it was a new motor he was dealing with and all it needed was the wire re-soldering onto the fitting.

The Company Man continued to follow various paths of excuse to fit a new motor until Lochinvar realised that his need to get on outweighed the determination to press the point. At this stage he did, unwillingly, accept that the man wanted to fit a new motor but that all the proud new father wanted was the wire to be reattached and that was all he was prepared to pay for. Company Man went out to his van, fetched a new motor and fitted it. His joy was almost unbounded when it worked. Lochinvar made the point that of course it worked and that the same result would have been accomplished by his own proposal. Company Man was not a person to allow anyone else's point to override his own and maintained his enthusiasm until it came the time to sign for the work. New father simply refused and added a note on the worksheet to the effect that all he had required was a wire reattaching to the existing new motor. Company Man and dissatisfied customer parted company for a period that both hoped would never end.

Three months later new father received a bill from the Electricity Board for £114:28. He refused to pay, offering the £14:67 – the labour element. This continued back and forth until they offered to take him to court. He accepted. They in turn replied with a threat that he could well be required to serve a prison sentence for this. Having managed to avoid prison thus far he considered this and responded to say "See you in court". The day of the appearance dawned and at the appointed hour young father made his way to the courtroom. Having registered his presence with the Registrar he sat in a room, quite peacefully and cool, to await the time of his trial. A man, a complete stranger to him, came in and sat down. After a couple of minutes he asked after the young father's name. He wasn't going to fool anyone that easily so Lochinvar asked why. He was from the Board and reminded father of the serious nature of his crime and that he could face a sentence for it. Lochinvar reminded him of his position and that he would sue them for defamation of character, wasting police and court time and for damages if they continued.

Company Legal Eagle looked thoughtful for a minute and then said "In that case, we are prepared to accept your offer of £14:67 for labour.

They were called up to the registrar who asked if we had managed to speak. The Board spokesman said they had and explained that they had accepted the original offer. The registrar looked at him for a couple of seconds and then, in a low but meaningful voice, said "I think you are very wise".

Case dismissed.

The Ranters

There is a poem, one I recall from my childhood, that starts "When fishes flew and forests walked and figs grew upon thorn, one moment when the moon was blood then surely, I was born...". I loved this poem for its poetic artistry coupled with the vivid pictures it helped paint on my juvenile impressionable mind. I was similarly impressed by witnessing a few of the sermons – now sadly long out of fashion – delivered by the fervent, almost fanatical Primitive Methodist preachers ("The Prims"). A few of these were local lay preachers but did not allow any restrictions that this status conferred on them to affect their weekly attack on their poor unworthy congregations. They attacked with a vigour and a volume to match that had the poor unsuspecting captive audience quaking in their pews. The rural peasantry sat in awe as these Prims, as they were called, and Ranters, as they came to be dubbed, raised their voices with threats of dire sufferings for eternity in the fiery bowels of Hell itself.

"You are all sinners", was a popular introductory sentence "You will all burn in the fires of Satan", made the ashen faced trembling flock quite literally tremble with fear. And so, the age of the Ranters passed, although I do know of someone who regularly lectures on the riveting subjects of Geology and Geomorphology who occasionally reverts to utilising their tactics. It is a sign of a good lecturer who can hold their audience and read the state of it, then adjust their delivery accordingly. One cold winter's night some years past, the dismal pervading damp of the prevailing weather had, along with the generous warmth from an efficient heating system, developed by a happy marriage into a scientific 'Fugg' that was slowly rendering an otherwise attentive audience towards slumber.

The man at the lectern noticed the slow drooping of heads that betrayed a waning of attention and responded with a slick delivery. The topic was the transitional change within landscapes due to the increasing fluvial erosion of both soil and underlying rocks that so dramatically altered not only landscapes but whole country boundaries. Even as he saw the potential disaster, he was already forming a plan to recover his audience and suddenly, without warning, thumped his fist down onto the timbered face of the lectern and in a loud voice shouted, "and suddenly ..." the audience jumped, a few of the women shrieked in mock horror, a couple of the men started with a low expletive, but all were immediately intrigued by the concept of something happening suddenly and intrigued by what was possibly to come. After a second or two dramatic pause to allow the audience to recompose and settle, he went on "and when I say suddenly, I mean during the course of several hundreds of thousands of years...". The torpor had been broken, the potential to lose the audience averted and success guaranteed.

Life, especially if lived for every second, is never dull and another great example of the unexpected came to me along with this story. Peter (jacket changed to protect the sartorial) a good friend and fellow author, related a tale that bore a similar twist but in totally different vein.

As a young recent Methodist Local Preacher he had been asked to lead a service and preach in a tiny village chapel deep in the heart of rural Kent. Having grown up a 'Saaff Lannonner' he was unused to the soft burr of the Garden of England and was advised by other, more experienced, clergy on how to structure the service to allow for the more rural nature of the clientele and their capacity for English "as she is spoke". As the great day approached, he ran through his service sheet, making a few improvements which he felt might improve his performance and the enjoyment of his congregation. A sudden and unexpected downpour of snow, the product of an untimely and unexpected cold snap, saw several inches of unfamiliar white delivered to the whole countryside and daily temperatures remaining stubbornly below zero. Nothing daunted he looked out his old long john combinations and thermal vest, donned a pair of extra thick trousers, their previous occupant betrayed by the presence of a truncheon pocket, and two woollen jumpers below a strong winter coat with hood bearing tell tale signs of its naval heritage.

Satisfied with his precautions against the elements he dutifully pedalled off towards his glory (or doom), arriving outside the little chapel almost coincidentally with the Duty Church Steward (a post I know well). This man was also a full time farmer and had worked hard all day tending to his stock and foddering his cattle, despite the inclemency. They exchanged muffled greetings and entered the little chapel. Someone had thoughtfully lit the old cast iron boiler and the room was pleasantly warm. As the time for the service began and no other being appeared, Peter suggested that "Since we have made the effort, should we just do a few readings and some prayers?" This was agreed and he set off with a couple of Bible readings that he considered appropriate for the current inclemency. This he followed with a series of carefully headed and well thought out prayers, halfway through which, as he paused for breath that would help develop the dramatic effect, he sensed rather than noticed a low slow snoring sound. Opening his eyes, a little and looking up from his lap he devised that the sole member of his congregation, the old caretaker, had succumbed to the comfort of the chair and had fallen asleep.

Intrigued by this development I asked for what we silently prayed would be a suitably dramatic conclusion to the story. Peter just shrugged in his own inimitable style and casually said "Well there was little I could do and was too impolite to waken him, so I just got dressed and quietly let him remain there asleep.

He's probably still there".

Christmas Eve

You see, there was this girl, well woman really but, in certain cases, where they look so vulnerable, girl somehow seems more appropriate. Anyway, she was sitting outside a bank on Iron Gate in Derby being steadfastly ignored by the long steady train of humanity busily collecting payouts from the cashpoint. She had a small pinched face that exhibited a distinctly cold appearance. She made no effort to ask for money and in three times of my passing over a period of an hour no one appeared to give her any. By the time I plucked up the courage to speak she seemed close to falling asleep. "I'm just going outside – and may be some time" I remembered from Scott's last voyage. The feeling of wanting to go to sleep is one I have experienced in extreme conditions. The knowledge of how it could develop frightens me, so I squatted down beside her.

"Would you like something to eat?" I started. Her voice was soft and positive. "Yes I would, very much". On the way over to the Market Place I discovered that she had been living with someone for three years and that he beat her regularly with more enthusiasm each time. She was thirty-five. She looked about fifty.

I gave her the full run of the menu. She chose modestly and wisely "Liver and onions please". She thought the offer of fruit juice was the alternative so declined. She drank it in one go when I got it anyway. She considered the coffee to be the best she had ever tasted. In her position I am sure I would have too. She ate with something approaching desperation despite me advising her to go slow. She talked about her family, father 86 years old in a flat in a suburb and unable (or unwilling) to take her in. A sister in Derby not prepared to let her stay. Her brother was her real goal. He then lived in Berwick-on-Tweed and she spoke with warmth and confidence about staying with him if only she could get there.

Her glove was her purse (for safety) and she searched through coppers, eyes lighting up with obvious spontaneous delight at finding a pound coin, for a twenty pence piece to ring her sister. I was right. She could only eat some of the dinner. She apologised to me for wasting it, suggesting her stomach had shrunk. It was the first hot meal she had eaten for three days. She spoke of the three of them sharing a garage in Derby. "This is no way to spend Christmas" she said, crying as she did. I told her to shut up before I started. It was very close.

She kissed me lightly on the cheek and gave me a look as if she was going to add something, then changed her mind.

As I left I thought about the office party and how lucky I was to leave just at the right time. Another five minutes and I may have missed her. Her name is Stephanie. She does not know it but I know the bloke she was living with. He deserves to be alone.

I got probably the best present I remember for a year or two this lunch time, to see someone really appreciate a really small gift, a lunch in Acropolis.

Happy Christmas everyone.

Mara and Me

I had just returned from the burial service of an old friend when this thought occurred to me, that I never would have had so much fun and enjoyment in the Maasai Mara as I did without him in tow. It began simply enough one day when my wife and I were discussing the prospects of a return visit (for me the third) to Kenya. On our previous trip we had undertaken a three day Safari to the Maasai Mara, that wonderful game reserve in the South West of the Country and abutting the great Serengeti, itself situated on the Northern border of Tanzania. On that occasion we had seen most of the wildlife but, despite all the best efforts of our guide and driver, no sign of either Leopard or Rhino. I was hoping that this visit might rectify that.

A deep gravelly voice at my elbow suddenly started "If oi was to offer to cam to Keenya (he was from another time) with you would oi be considered an incumbrance aand a thorough nuisance?". I thought it only polite to both answer and be honest. "Of course you would Lou," I began, but before I could continue or complete my insults he quickly chipped in "Good, in that caise oi'll cam along". The gravelly South of the Thames accent belonged to Lou Stevens. He was then ninety years old, with some interesting medical history and an ability to mistakenly rub people up the wrong way, purely by manner of his straightforward approach and voice. Luckily we had got on quite well with each other for many years and he regularly would interrupt another conversation to say to someone close by "I hate this man, I really loath him" and so our relationship developed along these lines. What Lou was really asking I suspected was, "would I be a liability that you are prepared to risk, taking a man of my age on a not altogether easy or completely safe trip". I did think it over for a short while but on consideration dismissed my selfish thoughts with one of some pride that he had chosen to risk his own safety and comfort to me, a man he publicly admitted to loathing.

We flew from Birmingham via Charles de Gaulle (a not too enjoyable adventure all on its own), arriving in Nairobi as the hot sweet sultry slightly rank air of midnight in Africa approached. I had already primed Lou not to make any undue clever, rude or contentious comments until we were well out of the airport, since his diplomacy could at times be wanting. Like a fool I had related my own experience on arrival at my first trip and did not want a repeat at any cost. We should not have worried. A man from Customs shepherded us towards a long table and asked where we were going and why. Having learned from experience I simply told him "We are coming to help a Bishop build a school and orphanage". The response was simple and immediate. He rather generously waved us through with no further examination.

Later the following day Lou and I were speaking about our proposed itinerary. Quite suddenly Lou started "You know what Ian, I took out some good insurance with no problem before I came. I hope I die whilst we are here". I listened with some surprise and more than a little concern and asked why on earth would he want to do that. Not phased at all by this comment so far he continued, "Well when I looked in detail at the policy it turns out that if I die out here they will repatriate the body at their expense. So I will get my money's worth." I managed a wry smile at this since one never knew just how serious or frivolous his comments might be. I had no need to worry, he was not the sort of person to allow a little thing like that to interfere with him having a good time.

We repeated our Mara safari, once again visiting the Maasai village where old acquaintances greeted us with huge smiles and crushing hugs. We faced the usual greetings of the males jumping dance, the show of the lion's mane headdress, the offer of trinkets specially made for tourists and not worth a light and then something really worthwhile, I bought a pair of Michelins. Now when I say that I really mean a pair of traditional Maasai sandals carefully constructed from old worn-out Michelin tyres. Although not that comfortable to some I gratefully discovered that they fitted me rather well and I was able to wear them without any discomfort or getting blisters. This, combined with managing to see my two remaining species that I missed on the first trip, Rhino and Leopard, made it another lovely trip and despite spending our nights in tents with all the wild animals running free close at hand it felt both comfortable and secure.

The highlights of driving around the reserve were too many to consider listing but two of the most memorable were:- getting out in a secure place with plenty of long range views all round for a picnic and, the most entertaining at least, as we were all engaged in photographing seven lionesses busily using their energy resting in the shade of a thorn bush, Lou asking me almost politely "Ian, would you mind just getting out and standing over there with those animals, it would make a really great photo." Sadly he did not get his photograph and may just live to regret coming with me after all.

In the event even this was denied him and I do sometimes wonder if he died cursing me for his bad luck.

Scab

Gerry Murphy was not a standard bog Paddy. Short, rotund and extremely talented, I met him on site when he was Steel Fixer Foreman. His skill with selecting bars to minimise waste was legendary, matched only by his consummate skill in both bending and fixing. His self confessed failures lay in his personal and family life where he regularly admitted to his lack of ability to control both his darling wife and their ever growing brood of children. Not that he was a bad father, far from it, he doted on his kids, despite their seeming life plan to upset and embarrass him and his wife at every opportunity. Many, regular and increasingly perturbing, were the letters from school, often commencing "your presence is requested at ..." and he became at his wits end towards the end of term – any term, when the various pranks and japes that were able to be identified as originating from a fertile Murphy mind could be proven.

The youngest, Michael, appeared to be breaking the mould for a while but the old genes came through with a vengeance half way through his second year at Senior school and his versatility at upsetting the staff rapidly progressed at an astonishing rate as the year dragged by. During one term he was recorded as 'absent' on more occasions than 'present' and almost all due to being ordered rather than requested not to return until sent for. He was of course a hit with the girls, who admired his courage to stand up to even the most feared of teachers. He was also – or at least appeared to be – fearless and once he had heard it he liked the term so much, it stuck. Mick the Fearless he became known as wherever he went. This of course was a hard act to live up to. As a consequence, he regularly sustained tumbles and falls resulting in a whole variety of cuts, scrapes, grazes and bumps, all of which added to his charisma with the fair sex. He did not appear to notice, there were far more important things on which to concentrate the mind.

During one particular term Gerry was almost at his wits end with young Fearless, with whom he ran a constant battle. He walloped him with a slipper, his belt, a stick and on one occasion, in an attempt to bring him round through deprivation if not desperation, locked him away in his bedroom. Fearless simply opened the window and lightly dropped to the floor, spraining an ankle and gaining even more credibility with the *vox popularis*.

Gerry continued to regale the site office with tales of young Fearless, his exploits, his successes and even his failures. Nothing, it seemed, would turn him away from his disruptive ways, but Gerry was not a man to give up lightly.

During one particular stunt that went spectacularly wrong, Fearless managed to sustain a long deep cut to his forehead that needed stitches and, as the doctor said, "Will almost certainly be a permanent lifelong scar". Fearless was ecstatic. It became for him the equivalent of the duelling scar and he proudly combed his hair out of the way so everyone could witness his latest acquisition. Gerry was not amused and ordered him to help tidy and clean the house and to wash up after all meals for a week. He expected some explosion of revolution. Nothing came. He waited in vain for the rebellion that never materialised. Fearless it seemed was now content with his lot, along with the undying admiration of the whole school. Michael it appeared had at last found himself a niche with which he was content.

Gerry found himself looking again at his errant son. He was good looking, in a Murphy sort of way, he had really made progress in class, even gained teacher stars and written comments on the quality of his work. Something was seriously wrong and Gerry was going to get to the bottom of it. After several attempts to find out he was now wondering where he could turn next. His wife simply kept saying "leave him alone and he will surprise us all" but that was not enough. Gerry tried – unsuccessfully – to upset young Fearless, but the prodigal was, it seemed, not for turning and blithely continued to plough his straight and narrow furrow through life.

The father was now becoming the ridicule of the household. Everyone knew that he was trying his best to get the better of Michael, just as a matter of principal and that just added fuel to the already white hot conflagration that churned within Gerry's belly. One day, young Fearless (even Gerry had become to think of him as this nowadays) had done an especially lovely thing for an old lady who lived locally and refused to accept any reward but her thanks. Gerry was clearly moved and relayed the story to us all, with genuine tears in his eyes. He told of how he had put the children to bed but had ordered young Michael to look after himself but, having sorted all the others, could not resist looking in to see how he was. Apparently he was doing rather well and appeared to be already asleep. Gerry wandered across and saw the angelic face of his son gently breathing away deep in peaceful slumber. He could not resist bending down and giving the lad a gentle kiss on his forehead. He genuinely thought he had won the day. As he turned to leave the bedroom Michael spoke –

"Dad",
"Yes son".
"You just kissed my scab".

Taming the Untamable

It had been decided that a training week end – designed mostly around the new and inexperienced expedition members – should be held. Wales seemed like a sensible place, particularly since it was the middle of Winter and the forecast was for sleet and snow with a portion of gales thrown in absolutely free.

The drive across was uneventful bordering on drear so with heater and windscreen wipers on, the only thing worth doing was grumble the whole time. For a crowd of fairly seasoned Arctic travellers we appeared less than enthusiastic let alone suitable candidates. But all that was to change. We camped in the Llewelyn mountains in an area less boggy and with fewer surface streams than most and waited for nightfall, praying that the pegs would hold, the poles would not snap and the tents would not leak. Of course they wouldn't. Would they?

In the cold misty half light of the following afternoon (the morning had proved too wet to be useful) with a nasty North Westerly wind rising to force "hard to walk upright!" we set off as a band to undertake some simple navigation for the newcomers and some crevasse rescue practice for the rest. We may gloss over the next four hours, since they are neither germane nor interesting and so we arrive smoothly at the time to go home for tea.

The Group Leader suddenly drew me to one side and said to me, "Ian, see that ridge to the North, go up there and find a suitable place for a rescue for tomorrow, then meet us at camp". Oh joy, it was something like half a mile away, the ground appeared to be undulating and covered with Ling (wild heather). Ling that is unmanaged grows up to a couple of meters long and its twisted stems forms traps for even the most of wary travellers. Oh deep, deep joy.

By the time I reached the foot of the escarpment I could pick out a series of steep (some very) gullies. None appealing. I chose one at random and set off climbing. At this point the wind, which had, up to now, remained a steady force six and head on started to build. When I say build, it was more of a sudden demented avalanche, crashing down the gully making the uncontrollable undergrowth thrash about like possessed things. Fronds of bracken ripped across my face leaving tell tale marks, clods of peaty earth rained down onto my head and what felt like small cauldrons of freezing water cascaded after them, putting headgear and hood to severe test. The further I climbed the steeper the gulley and less secure my position, until I was seriously considering aborting my mission in favour of a selfish decision for survival. Just then I thought I could see the top and the end of the climb so plumped for continue. I almost lived to regret it.

The wind which, up to now, had been slowly increasing in force and fury took on another dimension and suddenly rose in a demonic crescendo to a primeval scream so loud and so frightening that I could do nothing but hang onto my position and tremble in pure fear. After what seemed like a minute or two but was probably in reality a few seconds the storm took a short breath and during the comparative lull I heard myself scream out "No, please stop it, I'm a friend". I suddenly felt a fool, looking round in case some other idiot was around. There was no one but the mountain, the wind and me. At that moment I felt like kneeling down and offering a short prayer for my salvation. In the end, I just looked up and very quietly said a heartfelt and earnest "Thank you". The wind died, the evening sun appeared and I left the hill.

Never listen if anyone ever tries to tell you the earth is not a living breathing thing. That day I swear it listened to me and, luckily for me, answered. Not in the grandeur of the storm but in the quiet stillness that followed.

Now where have I heard that one before?

Mechanical Disadvantage

It would be around March of 1960 when I acquired my very first car. I had sort of inherited it from a cousin, who in turn had himself managed to obtain another. Note the absence here of the buy word, as in those days and times, exchanges frequently took place, a sort of local barter system. Anyway, it was a 1947 Ford Popular in a delicate shade of mushroom. I had not long passed my driving test, something I managed to do first time, despite having learned predominantly on wrecks of vehicles and latterly a One Ton Bedford van. This last was the worst of all, since it had column gear change, a system that made gear selection a lottery and felt as if one were stirring a rice pudding. Successful attainment of a desired gear was an occasion for celebration and often met with cheers – unsuccessful attempts by jeers.

I recall that one plan to seduce a lovely creature into my clutches began with an invitation to share a picnic with me at a local beauty spot, admire the stately home and observe the rowing races taking place on the river. All this was met with an unexpected acceptance and by chance, the day dawned fair. Now in those days one could open up the bonnets (wow, an access either side) to reveal an engine compartment where certain items were both visible and accessible. Not only that, identifiable as well. Just as well since, as we rolled along oblivious to the trials and tribulations ahead, I little thought how things would turn out. A couple of miles down the road I lost all power and was reduced to coasting along on tick-over. It was not the first time that this had occurred, so I was half prepared.

The accelerator system on these cars was operated by a rod system that contained fourteen joints. These were ball and socket type, which showed signs of wear very quickly, with the result that one or other often popped out. I quickly reassured my passenger that all was well, confidently climbed out, lifted the offside bonnet, made the connection, climbed back in and set off, me thankful, she in giggles. 10 miles further and the sun, that great white ball of fury, hung in a celestial powder blue sky, had all but disappeared behind skeins of light, but definitely grey, cloud. No matter, it was fine and mild, all the better for racing. Within five minutes more the light cloud cover had thickened to a leaden blanket. Soon, large drops of rain turned to huge globules that reduced visibility to near nothing. This was quickly followed by a series of small short screams from the object of my desires which alerted me to a problem. Spurts of water, forced up through holes in the floor, were jetting up her bare legs, to her chagrin and my embarrassment. We stopped. In the lay-by I found a large sheet of cardboard and managed to fashion a sort of deflector, forcing it gently into place, to direct the water away from bare flesh. Rain continued unabated, the windscreen wipers managing to keep some of it at bay. I cheerfully spoke of passing phase and fine afternoons to come. Her giggling had stopped.

That was when the wipers stopped too. In desperation so did I. These wipers were powered by a single electric motor sited above the driver's head, after the later style of those in a Land Rover. A small arm deployed them manually and the two wipers were joined by a short light metal arm. The necessity for ease of movement meant a certain looseness of the system and a short delay occurred between driving and driven sides. In addition to this the springs designed to hold them onto the windscreen had sprung so were no longer effective. In a crosswind, they wiped away happily, a couple of inches off the screen, tantalisingly efficiently, frustratingly ineffective. In order to continue I begged of my paramour to assist by reaching her arm across and winding the arm backwards and forwards to clear the screen. To her credit and after putting on my jacket, she accepted this proposal and complied.

All went well for a mile or less when, with a bang rather than a whimper, the exhaust fell off. By dint of good fortune, the torrential rain had abated so fell now only as a light drizzle. This helped me to avoid complete saturation as I scrabbled about underneath the car trying to secure the errant system with a handy length of wire. Having nothing handy in the way of chassis or frame on which to fasten this, I passed it through a hole in the floor. All I had to do now was to persuade my more than willing helper to wrap this around her hand and hold the end tight. We set off once again, me, peering through a misty windscreen, she, feet held up high out of the small fits of water that still found their way into the passenger well, right hand above my head operating the windscreen wipers, left hand holding a piece of wire that was gradually becoming warmer.

The remainder of the day passed relatively uneventfully, although the racing was poor and I subsequently failed to make the intended impression on little miss and did not get a return opportunity.

The next girl I fancied and took out, we went by 'chauffeur driven stretched limo', A number 27.

Mechanical Disadvantage

⤙ ⤚

Part the Second

It was around the time that the girls, with whom I had hoped to associate, began making excuses in favour of being transported to events with someone else that it dawned on me that my cars were not admired by all. Not that they were bland in any way, nor that they did not have character. Let's just get this straight; none of them ever had names. They were all metal boxes that got me from A to B – in theory. Admittedly, most of them did frequently get me away from A. Occasionally though not even that. On one infamous excursion the thing, for no apparent reason or justification, just stopped at a busy road junction and the two friends with me calmly got out and set off on foot. Not that I was unique in this situation.

On one grand occasion we were crawling through Mansfield traffic one mid-afternoon on market day. Traffic was solid, old ladies carrying shopping on their zimmers were overtaking us. Just then, the bloke lolling in the back seat, a really large lad, shouted out "Look there, someone has lost a wheel" as one gently rolled at an unsteady gait past us and down the road. As we leaned across to have a better look, the car lurched sideways and settled on one elbow, it was one of ours.

Naturally we had a spare wheel. Of course, it was flat. An old fashioned copper on point duty – white gauntlets and all – plodded his weary way, 'like schoolboy – unwillingly to school', towards us. "Now then lads, lets get this thing organised and gone shall we," he said – more out of hope than anger. My friend, the recent driver, looked embarrassingly bewildered "Er …" he began. The copper instinctively knew the rest "You don't have a jack do you?" once again, more a statement than a question, to be followed by "A wheel brace?" To the slow shake of my friend's increasingly crimson visage he strode up the road, stopping at the first four cars, ordering people out and commandeering them for higher things. For those of us just too young to remember the war but old enough to have seen first hand some of the results, it was just so exciting. Like old times, one could have said. Organising the four recruits into a unit, the policeman got three of them to lift up the offending vehicle. Then two more of us grabbed the side and helped hold it aloft. He then took the commandeered wheel brace and, just in time to remove the recovered wheel from the fourth (a red faced puffing billy who had spent two minutes chasing it past market stalls) he carefully removed one wheel nut from each of the remaining wheels and fitted the last one with the three recovered nuts. When all the excitement was over and the car was back four square he looked at us and slowly shook his head. We had nothing to contribute but a quietly delivered "sorry", whilst I secretly harbour the idea that he would write this up in his little black book – not as a criminal report or for future reference, but in order to retell it to the sergeant back at the station, over a mug of black tea, a toasted teacake and tearful laughter.

But, even at this stage, I had not forgotten how to make a little go a long way. The old fashioned engines – 1172cc Side Valve get up and go types, would almost run on anything, so since they were capable of it, I was prepared to try it. The disadvantage of a local garage was that the owners knew my family. Requests for 'two gallons of mixed please' were met with mock horror and some refusal, until, with sidelong glances up and down the street, he would ask "have you got a tin?" The affirmation of this would stimulate him into putting a gallon of petrol – best (around this time there were only two types, best and worst) into the car's fuel tank, then filling a one gallon jerry can with a gallon of paraffin (pink). He left me to empty the latter into the fuel tank. Once achieved I set off in an impressive cloud of strangely white smoke and the smell of a greenhouse, but unlike nowadays, it worked. It would be interesting to try mixing paraffin with petrol for a modern engine and see how it fared, although I have to declare, I did on one unforgettable occasion fill the car with petrol in Derby and set off towards Leeds. It was only when cars, vans, lorries and even a plastic pig overtook me on the M1 as I chugged uphill in second gear at 20 MPH that I remembered it was a diesel engine. Sadly the days of enjoyable, exciting, unpredictable driving seem to be over for good.

Even simple breakdowns now have sinister sides. It is with genuine tears of remembrance that I recall a friend who was forced to stop on one motorway due to a puncture. Whilst changing the wheel he was killed by a lorry whilst on the hard shoulder, the driver had fallen asleep at the wheel. He was 23 years old and in his last year of Dentistry. Somehow the loss to the World seems as criminal as the act itself.

Motoring has lost its spark and along with it, most of the fun. Still, it occasionally has its day.

Mechanical Disadvantage

-<- ->-

Part the Third

There comes a time in everyone's life when reflection is the only thing left. I remember thinking this as I looked into the engine compartment of my car. It was not that I did not expect to see what was in there, namely, an engine. No, it was that the thing I was observing was nothing like the engine I knew and loathed of old. I could not even see, find or identify any of the usual familiar parts with which I had spent so many happy hours fighting to fix, remove and replace on previous cars. All I could see was a huge block of metal that carried a conspicuous and impressive badge but told me nothing of its purpose. Admittedly I could see a dipstick, but strangely, no filler cap.

Of course with the advent of electronic ignition, turbo chargers, twin overhead cams, double triple expansion valves, intercoolers, mega-multipliers and other things I don't understand, I have become a victim of progress. But is it progress? Where is the opportunity to spend an enjoyable Saturday with a friend, a child, a willing wife lying underneath a vehicle, up to the elbows in dust, grease, oil, worse, eyes red rimmed with grime and dust, showing him / her / them just how to mess up a relatively simple operation like changing brake pads. There used to be a time when a really useful Mr Haynes produced a whole series of manuals that allowed anyone with a modicum of common sense to dismantle and rebuild almost an entire vehicle (this presupposes of course one had the requisite specialist equipment) but not any more. If Wordsworth were alive today he would possibly pen a short, terse little ditty called "Upon Lifting the Bonnet of my Car", or "Lines from my Engine Compartment". I find nowadays that I perform the bonnet lifting operation in order to act merely as a spectator, although I do from time to time fill the windscreen washer bottle. This itself used to be a matter of:- locating the old washing up liquid bottle rolling about somewhere in the depths of the drivers well, taking into the public toilets / pub / home, filling it with water, adding that certain *Je ne C'est quoi* and throwing it casually back into the car to slowly leak a weak solution onto the floor. Since this almost inevitably leaked, it was not too bad and at least kept the interior smelling less of humanity than of kitchen. Although all this sounds a bit of a moan, nothing could have prepared me for the latest trauma – or the outcome.

Following the last normal (if anything costing £300 can be termed normal) 10,000 mile service, I had noted a loss of power from my pride and joy. This became gradually more acute as days past. The time progressed but sadly I did not. I was expecting the performance commensurate with the rear of the car, that read something like "1.9TD EFI" or something similar. **Durthethingsalltechnic** of the adverts was nowhere to be appreciated. The lady driver of the household steadfastly passed no comment. I deliberately left her to observe and comment on just how bad it was but to no avail. No amount of frustration on my part could, it seemed, induce her to ask the question "What's wrong with the car?" During a run to Newark one evening with friends, I commented on this, suggesting that the Turbo may have stopped working. "Blimey" said Steve, a passenger, quite restrained I thought, "that sounds expensive". Days passed and it really was becoming quite dangerously underpowered. At length I could stand it no longer and, since I now admit to knowing nothing of these things, booked it in to be looked into. Now I have used this particular garage for many years. I like the owner and what is more important, I trust him. He had not commented on anything at the last service and I thought he perhaps might have done if he had either seen, heard, or suspected anything was going or had gone wrong. It appeared to me suddenly that we have accepted our car mechanics to be almost like doctors, with all their diagnostics machines. He looked at me poker-faced as I described the symptoms and signs. After a few moments he leapt into action like a coiled spring. "Make me a coffee" he ordered. Three minutes later, when I appeared with his favourite mug steaming away, he smiled that knowing smile and nodded across at the car.

"Have you found out what it is?" I asked, he nodded again towards it "It's ready for you" he said. I looked on with incredulity. He had not had the time to do anything. I had not heard the engine start, stop, cough, choke, rumble, anything. He obviously felt the building up of anxiety and frustration and quietly added the explanation. "You know how you replaced the carpets?" I did, "You know how you put an old one on top to protect the new one?" I did. "Well you trapped the top one under the accelerator". It now runs as it always has and feels like a new vehicle. Cars. Don't you just love them?

Does anyone know how you apply for a Gold Card?

In The Bag

The flight had been straightforward if boring but the walk from the aircraft into the airport building was something of a shock. After the relative cool of the cabin the fierce heat of the African night struck me like a physical blow as I began a completely new experience. The heat, the smell, the bodies, the clamour and more all combined to overwhelm the senses and I genuinely felt like a little boy lost in a gigantic store.

The feeling did not last long since I had more than this to think about. My 56 Kilograms of luggage had to be located and recovered, passport control had to be faced, possible problems with the access visa may occur and a host of ugly threatening looking people all could be there to rob me or worse. Luckily I soon pulled myself together and started to plan. Firstly I took heed of the locals and grabbed a trolley almost out of the hands of a lady with three small children in tow. I then tried to work my way to the front of the heaving mass that seemed to completely encircle the belt. This proved an impossible task and very quickly taught me a valuable lesson in dealing with this situation. Don't push against, use them to help you, spotting small cracks in the walls of bodies and slipping through to the next level, dodging around huge men and women all trying to get to the front.

All this was of course a fruitless exercise on their behalf but like most of humanity they had not thought it through. Following one slick move I felt quite like Super-Mario as I saw the actual luggage belt before me but soon realised that position is no good unless goods come into view. Mine it seemed were destined never to appear and so it was that twenty minutes later the rush was all over and just five of us stood around jealously guarding our acres of empty hall whilst the aged belt wheezed and groaned its way on a never ending circular route, like Sysiphus aimlessly pushing his boulder uphill in the Underworld.

At that very moment one shaft of light relief broke through the worry and anxiety as a single suitcase handle trundled its lonely way through the opening flaps and around the belt itself. I was close to bursting out laughing and more so a little later but managed to supress this and merely grinned internally to myself as the handle danced a slow rotating waltz along the belt. It approached one grim looking individual who, for reasons best known to himself, bent down and examined it, almost as if to see if it did belong somehow to his lost luggage. Believe me gently reader when I tell you at this stage I almost wet myself. I felt for a second or two that it was a real choice between that or internally haemorrhage as I tried my very best to keep control. Another ten minutes later, just as I was beginning to genuinely panic, my rucksack appeared, closely followed by the huge suitcase (handle attached) and third surplus bag containing mostly paper and school books. Anxiety gone I rushed forward for a second before taking new stock and looking round in embarrassment since there was now no competition.

Goods carefully loaded onto the trolley I sidled my way almost crablike thanks to the one mandatory frozen wheel and set off towards "Good to declare" exit. Not for me the risk of being clever in this new cloyingly sweet smelling foreign country, no, I would toe the party line. Internally I was praying I might get a friendly Customs Inspector who would merely smile, mark an exaggerated yellow cross on my things and wave me through. Stupid I know but one can always hope. As I entered the customs hall one sour faced individual gestured to me with what looked for all the world like a swagger stick. "Jas put it hover 'eer" he ordered waving his stick towards a long wooden bench. I did as I was told but did not attempt to lift anything off the trolley. I knew I was skating on thin ice but was determined to be treated with some sort of respect. Oh how the stupid can confirm their natural ability by the smallest of gestures. He looked long and hard at me then asked "Wat is in the baag?" as if he did not already know. I thought I might play the game so answered "You know what it is, this just went through the X-Ray machine". He looked more darkly than ever and rasped out "Are aall these tools noo?" Now I was prepared for this so quickly burst out laughing and said "of course not, they are old ones for me to use, I am here to help build a school for your children." At this he either changed his mind about me or simply realised he was dealing with a lunatic. Sighing slowly he extended his right arm and to my immediate joy and delight emblazoned my huge suitcase and accompanying rucksac with a vibrant yellow cross. I was elated and through.

Beyond the double doors towards freedom was a party of four huge Kenyan soldiers in camouflage uniforms and carrying some sort of sub machine pistols, made more sinister looking by way of a skeleton stock, presumably to aid long range killing. I knew I was drawing attention by my white skin and large cargo. This totally comprised one huge suitcase, one large rucksac, one laptop computer carrying bag, one medium cabin bag and a small stiff zip top bag. This last was slung over one shoulder by means of a long leather-look strap.

As I passed the last of the uniforms he looked at

me, gestured with the gun and asked "Waat is in the bag?" Another one asking the same question. Frankly I was not thinking, was too tired and could not stop myself as I heard a voice that turned out to be mine respond "Drugs". This was actually true since the little bag was full of aspirin and paracetamol for the local hospital. He looked at me for a split second before breaking into the widest grin and saying "Go on, go on", gesturing towards the exit with his gun. That night I did say my prayers and genuinely thanked God for his sense of humour and my pure luck, thanks mostly to my own gross stupidity.

On my subsequent trips to Kenya I decided not to employ this tactic.

Last Gasp

The bedside table took on a whole new dimension as the day went by. It had started as a receptacle for all the things he wanted and needed most. The remains of bunches of grapes slowly turning wizened and ever so slightly soft in their neglect. Paperwork that charted his detailed daily routine – now sadly no longer either needed or consulted, two books – potentially exciting but not even started. And his prize possession, his watch. A Rolex of course and one of several he had owned for some time. He was not in penury. Far From it.

As morning turned slowly towards lunch his active mind moved from picture to circumstance to memory to thought. The face of his long dead wife came into sharp focus and he wondered how things may have been different if only they had been able to start a family. He was not a man to accept that he would have been a good father but those who knew him, no, really knew him, thought differently. The low murmur of voices took him back to Canada and the parties they had enjoyed with others of the

Royal Canadian Mounted Police. He had done well
with his life, lived a lot. From 'London and the Met'
had come the offer for Kenya. It was a place he
had never really wanted to go and when he heard
of the life expectancy of a British bobby out there
just then (ten days – the Mau Mau were at their
height) he had at length decided and Canada had
been the result.

His mind wandered to another love of his life –
Angling. Some people called it fishing. He loathed
the wrong reference and had no time for those who
confused the two. He used to correct people in the
nicest possible way. "Anglers try to outwit a fish
with rod and line. Fishermen collect them in a huge
net with a boat". They used to laugh in scorn and
wonder to themselves how he thought he knew so
much. He used to think about which of his many
published books on angling would suit them. None
of them of course was the right answer.

As the day progressed in its monotonous routine
his mind wandered – times of deep joy, of sadness
of course but always tinged with hope and comfort.
His mouth was dry, very dry. His normal croaky
voice was reduced to a whisper and even that a
very quiet one. Not like him at all. He remembered
a chance meeting in a public toilet many years ago
now when he was approached and propositioned
by another man. He tried his best to persuade this
low life degenerate that he was not the one to be

asked. The man persisted. Not once, not twice but a third time and at last our man had simply had enough. He smiled a slow wry smile at the picture his mind conjured up as he, the approached, quietly expressed his regret but needing to put things right, then pulling out his warrant card he read the man his rights as the poor specimen looked on aghast before collapsing into tears of mock remorse as the 'cuffs clicked onto soft, overindulged and pulpy wrists.

As the evening drew on his thirst increased and his ability to let them know he needed a drink reduced. He lay patiently waiting for someone to arrive at his bedside. When they did it was not what he wanted. By then every bone in his body ached and his breathing had become laboured and shallow. He knew what was coming. His thoughts turned back to Kenya and his luck at getting there to visit the school he helped support. There he remembered meeting the young women of the teaching staff and how he delighted in asking his companion "How many cows for this one?" in mock sincerity of seeking a bride. He saw the young, pinched faces of the pupils, remembered some of the stories of them being rescued from a life with no prospects of a proper life and his determination to help.

He remembered with joy the three days of safari in the Maasai Mara. The jolting bumping discomfort of the ride. The constant remains of familiar animals, Wilderbeest, Zebra, Grants and Thompsons gazelle. The massive bulk and the slow delicate movement of Elephant, the pure elegance of the Cheetah, the huge bulks of Hippo' lying half in half out of the river and of course the Lion. By way of a deliberately controversial comment he made the point that the male did not have to hunt whilst he had all those pretty females to do it for him. We all laughed. Almost as an afterthought he looked across at the seven lionesses lying in various recumbent postures in the relative cool shade of a small bush and with an air of complete sincerity suggested "just get out and stand over by that bush will you, it would make a lovely photograph" then laughingly suggested I was quite selfish to not have complied.

The face was round and very black. She came quietly and made ready to move him to ICU, although at the time he neither knew nor cared. All he wanted was to take a few deep breaths and smell the complicated warm earthy and spiced aroma of Kenya. His breathing was laboured now and every breath he managed was an effort. The face came back into focus and her smile was warm and genuine. He thought of the teachers and how he had joked along with them over his mission in looking for a bride, for him of course he laughingly told them, as they stood smiling and shy. She was from Zimbabwe but he would never know that, as far as he was concerned she was doing something for his benefit and for that he was grateful and appreciative. He could hardly manage a breath now and tried to cry out as he felt himself being lifted and moved. He was on a ventilator and his breathing was being done for him. All he had to do now was to concentrate on the smiling black face that stroked his forehead and sat by his side. It was a real shame that no one was able to appreciate his sense of fun and adventure but if anyone had been listening to hear his final comment they would have heard him say with his last gasp "how many cows?"